Just How Long Is A Lifetime?

By D.A. Sciortino

Ink Smith Publishing

www.ink-smith.com

ISBN: 978-1-939156-93-8

Ink Smith Publishing
710 S. Myrtle Ave Suite 209
Monrovia, CA, 91016

I would like to dedicate this book to my family. For without them, I never would have pushed myself to finish. My husband and children are the most encouraging individuals I know and I am so very lucky to be a part of their lives.

To my extended family and friends, thank you all for being a positive influence. And finally, to Ink Smith Publishing, for giving me the opportunity to believe in myself.

Chapter 1

June 1933

Luisa had just finished packing away the last of her husband's clothes. It had been two months since Lorenzo passed away and the house seemed quiet without him there. She missed his deep voice calling for her. She even missed hearing him yell when things were not to his expectations. She put all his clothes in a box and put the cover over it. There was a knock on the bedroom door and she could hear it slowly opening.

"Hello? Luisa?" It was Luisa's daughter, Maria. "Are you alright?"

Luisa let out a long breath and her daughter came to sit next to her. "We all miss him," Maria sighed. She reached out and took an oval frame off the nightstand, tracing her fingers over her father's gray, wrinkled features. Luisa leaned on her daughter's shoulder and stared down at the picture of her husband, holding tightly to her hand. In the last fifteen or so years it had gotten difficult to go out in public and be the couple they had been. Luisa's features completely unchanged in their fifty years of marriage stared at her from the photograph.

"People thought he was my father for a time, I thought that was horrible to bear," Luisa muttered to her daughter. "But when they addressed me as his granddaughter – Maria, it broke my heart."

"I know, mama," Maria said, her voice tender. Tears sprang to Luisa's eyes. Maria, nor any of her children, had called her mama in years. Thinking long-term, the family decided it would make more sense to call her by her first name rather than try to explain the impossible to Luisa's grandchildren one day.

The impossible: Luisa never aged. Luisa looked no older than Maria – and never would.

Giuseppe, the eldest, Mario and Maria, the youngest, were on their way to becoming adults themselves and began asking more probing questions regarding their mother's appearance. When it became necessary for them to have a family discussion, more of an explanation, Lorenzo and Luisa sat their children down and told them their secret. Giuseppe was twenty-four when they told them, just ten years younger than their mother's physical appearance.

1

Lorenzo took the lead in their explanation. He said, perhaps this was part of God's plan and explained how this was not as wonderful as it seemed. To be young forever was a curse, to watch your loved ones grow old around you was not something that every person wished for. A curse, no one outside their family could know.

In fact, Luisa was experiencing the full effect of this curse now with Lorenzo's death. He was seventy-five years old when he died. As Luisa stood beside him, in his final weeks, she looked over at him each time with love in her eyes and yet, as visitors stopped by to express sympathy and good wishes, her youth cursed her.

In no way did she ever stop loving Lorenzo. Her heart grew old with him, her memories, her soul – but the outside did not change with it.

The children accepted the story, of course with many questions. None of them believed their parents but looking at their mother, she looked the same as always. Lorenzo did tell them that this was to be kept a secret and that nobody could ever know. As the children married and started families of their own, they decided to tell their spouses' at first their mother passed away and Luisa was introduced as their aunt, the younger sister of their mother's. As time went on Luisa still needed to show some signs of aging. She would mess her hair up before putting it up and even pat some dirt on her face. She gained some weight as hard as it was. She was always a slender woman but as Luisa gained a few pounds here and there, it became easier to eat more and more. Lorenzo didn't seem to mind. He said he would always love her no matter what she looked like. Of course, she had to move into another bedroom. They had to act a certain way in front of the new family members who all lived in the same villa. Luisa and Lorenzo would have their moments of privacy when everyone was busy tending to their own families.

Almost everyone called Luisa, Zia, which is aunt in Italian. Due to her age, she could not be called nonna, as she would have liked. Lorenzo was called nonno, which was fine because he was, in fact, their grandfather. However, even they were beginning to notice that Zia Luisa was not aging the way others around them did. They all swore it was because she never married and had children of her own. Little did they know.

"You should take these to your husband. They are still in good condition," Luisa said, pushing her husband's clothes towards her daughter.

"Mama, will you be alright?"

2

Luisa smiled at her daughter. She touched the crease between her daughter's eyes, a worry line Maria was born with. "I will be fine. I've come this far haven't I?"

Luisa's sons took over the vineyard and wine making business once Lorenzo became sick. Lorenzo taught them everything they needed to know.

****

After the family arrived in America 30 years prior, the business flourished. Lorenzo and his uncle worked day and night to optimize the vineyard – only three years later, Lorenzo's uncle passed away leaving Lorenzo to run the vineyard on his own. The family did well, but within 15 years, prohibition descended upon the country. Most of the vineyards closed down and some even ripped up their vines to plant other crops. Lorenzo refused.

He left his vineyards to grow and harvested as usual. He believed that one day it would all return and they just needed to be patient. Fortunately, they were able to rely on other sources of income during the drop in demand. Lorenzo grew olives to make oil and grew figs to sell. It all worked for the best. Shortly after prohibition, the demand for grapes was high – grapes were rare, and a ton of grapes, which used to cost $15 mounted to $80, $100, even $200. Lorenzo's vineyard, Messina Vineyard, was one of the only vineyards in California with grapes readily available.

Thankfully, Lorenzo was smart with the money he made at the time. People caught on and bought land and planted and planted. Not more than ten years later, the price for wine grapes dropped. Lower than they ever were. Supply was high but Lorenzo and his sons were smart. They did well for the family.

The vineyard was a beautiful place and over the years, they were able to expand the living quarters. All the children and their families lived on Messina Vineyard. It was a beautiful vineyard, even today.

Luisa watched her daughter tuck one of Lorenzo's crisp white shirts into box. She patted her mother on the shoulder, "All will be well, mama."

Maria left the room, and Luisa wrung her hands together. "For how long?" Luisa muttered to herself. She shook her head, Luisa was sure Lorenzo was looking down, proud of what he had accomplished. What *they* had accomplished together.

3

Chapter 2

It had been over a year since Lorenzo's death. Luisa was finding it difficult to fit in. The estate seemed to run just fine without her help. The children and their families were doing a great job.

She decided to take a walk through the vineyards one morning, right as the sun was rising. Lorenzo had built a bench for her for when they would take a walk together and needed a rest. Luisa sat on the bench and felt the cool air on her face. It was the quietest time of the day for her to enjoy. There were no workers talking and no children screaming and playing. She always enjoyed taking a walk that time of the day, before everyone else was out and ready to work. A perfect time for reflection.

1887

It seemed like yesterday when I was playing in the vineyard that my family worked at in a town called Salemi, in Sicily. I always had to help my mother in the kitchen very early in the morning. As soon as I was done, I would run around the vineyard, delighting in the sunshine. My father didn't like when I did this, he worried that he would be reprimanded for his children misbehaving.

As I got older, he didn't mind as much since I would just walk around, not run, and he knew I would not cause any trouble. One day, when I was seventeen, I decided to go out for my early walk. It was a time for me to have some privacy from the rest of the vineyard. As I was about to pick a bushel of grapes, I sensed someone close behind me. I turned quickly to see a boy who seemed close to my age, maybe a year or two older. I was taken aback by his wavy brown hair, light brown eyes, and a smile that quirked up at the corner – making any girl melt.

"I'm so sorry to disturb you. I was just going for a walk." He motioned towards me but stopped when he saw I was nervous. "My name is Giovanni. My family just started to work

4

here two days ago and I was just looking around before the day became busy." He seemed apologetic.

It was then I remembered hearing there was going to be a new family working on the vineyard so I assumed he was telling the truth.

"My name is Luisa. We work on the vineyard as well. Welcome." I couldn't look at him as much as I wanted to. My hands were actually shaking from nerves, although there was something about his demeanor that made me very comfortable. Perhaps it was his soft voice. My legs felt wobbly. I just stood there hoping he would say something but he didn't for a moment and there was a long awkward pause.

Thankfully, he finally said, "Luisa, it's very nice to meet you. I hope I will see you more often." I looked up at him, mesmerized by his smile before he turned and walked away. I couldn't stop watching him. He then turned back to look at me, still smiling as he continued on his way.

That day was not my best day as far as helping around the house. My mother had to yell at me numerous times. She would ask me to clean something and had to repeat it until I snapped out of the dream I was in.

"What has gotten into you, Luisa?" She was starting to get annoyed with me until it all came together in her mind. Giovanni had walked by and waved to me saying hello. I blushed like a dry red wine, and it was then that my mother knew.

That night my mother came to me after everyone had washed up for bed as she always did to brush my hair before I went to sleep. I loved when my mother brushed my hair, it was very soothing.

"You know, I remember being your age and the first time I saw a certain boy. He made me so nervous every time he was near." She laughed at the memory. "Luisa, you are getting older now and your father and I have talked about your future."

I knew what she was getting at. My family already had plans for the boy I was to marry. Lorenzo was a hard worker and the son of the vineyard's owner. The trouble was I never had a reaction to Lorenzo, like I did upon meeting Giovanni.

My mother was finishing with my hair. "We only want what is best for you Luisa. Always know that." She then gave me a kiss on my forehead, and tucked me in.

It didn't matter what my mother said. Giovanni was the boy I was going to daydream about.

The next day I finished my early morning chores and ran into the vineyard hoping Giovanni had the same idea. I didn't even realize how fast I was going until out of nowhere I banged into someone. That someone was Giovanni and it caused me to fall to the ground.

He turned suddenly almost falling himself. "Oh my goodness! Luisa, are you alright? I'm so sorry!" He was helping me up off the floor and just the touch of his hand made me want to cry with delight.

After sharing a laugh about crashing into each other, we started to walk together.

"So how long has your family been working here?" he asked.

"As long as I can remember. My father was friends with the owner of the vineyard growing up. They have known each other for a long time now. What about you? Where did you live before coming here?"

"Not too far from here. At first I wasn't happy with moving but I'm starting to change my mind." He looked up at me and smiled.

All I kept thinking about was how happy I was that he bumped into me the previous morning and not any of the other girls. Otherwise, they would be walking with him right now instead.

"You know, my father would not be very happy if he saw us here together." I thought it was fair to warn him.

"Why is that? He already plans on giving you to someone else?" he laughed.

All I could do was manage a look at him, which answered his question.

"Oh. Well in that case we should be careful. That is, if we plan on seeing each other often."

I was thinking of what my mother had said to me the previous night. It was more of a warning not to start liking another boy; Lorenzo was the one I was going to marry. I knew how important it was for my father and his position at the vineyard. I would never jeopardize anything involving my family, but I also did not see the harm in enjoying some time with Giovanni as well. It was harmless enough, just two friends enjoying a morning walk together.

Each day on our walk, I learned something new about him. He carried around a notepad, each page filled with scenes of the vineyard, women working in the kitchens, even children playing amongst the grape vines. Occasionally, a picture had some color to it, but most were just pencil sketches. He really knew how to capture their emotions, whether it was with laughter or a hard day working.

"Giovanni these are wonderful. Has anyone told you that you should be a professional artist?" I could not stop looking at all the sketches.

He chuckled. "No. My parents think there are better things in life to do. They said drawing will not make money for the family."

He seemed disappointed.

"How did you get into drawing?" I was genuinely curious.

"I'm not sure when I started drawing, but years ago we had family friends visit us for a few weeks. The father, Antonio, was an artist, nobody famous. He gave me some of his supplies when he saw how good I was at drawing. He told me if my parents did not let me make a life out of this, that I should still keep drawing. He said, I had too much talent to waste, and that I should draw whenever I had spare time. That wasn't much since my father has me working so hard, but I always find time. That's how much I love it."

7

This was just another reason for me to like him.

Months went by fast and during this time Giovanni and I spent a lot of time together, mostly in the morning but soon we found time at night after dinner as well. Sometimes my friends would help me out by pretending to be with me when I was really with Giovanni in case my parents asked.

One evening, we decided to meet after dinner by the old big tree, down the hill behind the house. When I arrived it was so dark that I started to get nervous being out there all alone. As I got closer to the tree, I heard branches breaking as if someone was walking on them, and I wondered if maybe it wasn't the best idea to be out here. Out of nowhere, Giovanni jumped out from behind the tree. I was so startled I thought I would cry. Noticing my expression, Giovanni came over and hugged me, still laughing.

"Oh Luisa, I'm sorry! I was just being playful." He chuckled once more and kissed me gently on the cheek, wrapping his hands around my waist in apology.

I froze. I wasn't sure exactly how I was feeling in that moment, but what I did know was that I did not want it to end.

His face stayed close to mine as our cheeks gently touched. He kissed me again, this time closer to my ear. Then again, closer down my jaw. He must have felt me shaking because he pulled back just a bit and looked me in the eyes.

"Luisa, I really like you a lot." Then he kissed me on the lips, very gently. It didn't last long as he clearly did not want to take advantage – but I wanted that moment to last.

"Come on, let's head back." He took my hand into his as we walked towards the house holding hands all the way. I marveled at the warm sensations traveling up my arm from his fingers, and felt the cold immediately rush back as soon as we untangled our fingers. Once we were in sight of the houses, we had to walk separately.

We met like these for weeks, stealing kisses when no one was watching and holding hands in the dark. But one day, my brother saw Giovanni and I holding hands behind the barn.

"Home, Luisa," he yelled. His face was livid – and as I walked away, casting a last glance of apology at Giovanni I saw the fear on Giovanni's face. I was promised to Lorenzo, Giovanni was not who my father wanted me to marry.

My family was only looking out for my future I suppose, but it still upset me that I could not marry for love.

The next morning, Giovanni met me in the vineyard to tell me he and his family were leaving. He did not say it was because of me, he didn't have too. I could tell by his face that I was. I was so upset to see him leave.

Giovanni held both of my hands in his and told me I would see him again one day. He promised. Then he kissed me gently on the lips. As he started to walk away, our hands still touching, I realized he had a left a paper in my hand. When I couldn't see him anymore, I looked down at the paper. It was a quick drawing of a young girl sitting on the grass. He had drawn me.

Later that night, my mother came into my bedroom. She didn't say anything, just handed me a glass of warm milk and brushed my hair. She always had a romantic side to her, and she had known my heart was breaking.

"Sometimes we need to make choices in life that we don't like, Luisa. I know that right now you don't understand why things happen the way they do but you need to trust your father. He only wants what is best for you. Lorenzo is a nice boy and he will take very good care of you. Always remember, nobody can take away what is inside of you, in your heart and the memories in your head."

Later that night, I went to bed, my eyes swollen from crying. It was only a day and already I missed Giovanni. He was all I could think of that night and remembered what my mother told me, that the memories could never be taken away from me. Memories of walks in the vineyard with Giovanni, the pictures he would draw and his silly behavior that always made me laugh.

Weeks passed, months even. Eventually I kept busy helping my mother in the kitchen. I was getting older and more mature. Lorenzo would sit next to me at dinner many nights. He started to ask if I would like to take a walk with him. Of course, we were never alone when we did this. Lorenzo turned out to be a nice boy. He was very shy but very determined which I started to admire. He would tell me his dreams of going to America.

"I would like to take you with me one day Luisa. I hope this is something you would like." He looked at me with his big brown eyes. Lorenzo had very strong features unlike Giovanni who was softer.

I started to fall in love with Lorenzo. I guess my mother was right, it seemed Lorenzo *would* be good to me and take care of me.

We were married two years later and moved into a different section of the house. Now, I lived amongst the family. Everyone treated me a little differently, with more respect. Lorenzo and I still took our walks, and as time went on – age and pregnancy would keep me from going too far. I remembered the first day that Lorenzo showed me the bench he built me. It was directly in the middle of the vineyard.

Sometimes after the children were in bed, he and I would sit on the bench together, holding hands and enjoy the fresh air and quiet.

Chapter 3

"Boun giorno signora." Luisa was brought back to reality by Marco, one of the workers. She smiled at him and got up from the bench. Luisa sometimes forgot how young she looks to everyone else. Men still looked at her a certain way. In her mind, she sometimes felt like she was in her sixties, which is what she should be. Luisa started to head back to the house. Her daughter in law, Franca had already made espresso. Luisa walked into the kitchen and poured herself a cup sitting down at the wooden table.

It had gotten to a point where Giuseppe had to tell the spouses what was going on. They were told the same story that Lorenzo and Luisa told their children which wasn't much. It was beyond believable but Luisa was proof enough. They all agreed not to talk openly about it.

"Did you enjoy your walk today, Luisa?" Franca was feeding her children breakfast. She was Giuseppe's wife and a good woman who always worked hard and was a great mother.

"Yes, thank you, Franca," Luisa replied.

"Luisa!" Giuseppe, her eldest son, came in the kitchen and kissed everyone on the cheek including Luisa. "How are you this morning?"

Giuseppe was the loud one in the family. Always talking loud, laughing loud and definitely yelling loud. He sounded just like his father. They had the same deep, strong voice. His voice showed everyone he was in charge that was for sure. She had to admit that Giuseppe was great at what he did. Even now, during the hard times of the depression, he still kept the family business strong. They had to cut back on many things but she knew that everything would be fine with him in charge.

Franca was cleaning up the dishes and held her hand out to the children to come with her to wash up.

"Giuseppe, I think I need an escape," Luisa said, while looking down at her cup knowing this was a hard thing to say. She could feel his eyes on her and sensed the confusion.

"What do you mean 'escape'?" She sometimes felt that Giuseppe started to treat her as if she was his little sister and not his mother. It was hard to talk down to him as he got older, he was strong minded like his father. Now that Lorenzo had been gone, Giuseppe had

11

been in charge of not only the vineyard but the family as well. Even more strange was that he was ten years older physically than Luisa was.

"The children will start to notice that I am not getting much older. How can you explain this to them? Your wives look at me as if there is something strange with me! They are supposed to be younger than me and yet I look better than they do!" She quickly recovered from that one. "Well, I mean not better but younger."

"You cannot go anywhere; you need to stay here with your family Luisa. This is where you belong. Do not worry about those silly things." He seemed upset with her request, quickly drinking his espresso and paying no mind to her.

"I can go live with your cousin Angelo for a little. I am sure they could use help at the store. It's a change for me." Angelo was not really her immediate relative. He was their uncle's nephew from his wife's side. When they first moved to California, they would spend a lot of time with their uncle and his wife's family because they were the only other family they had in America at the time. They lived almost two hours away and owned a meat and cheese store in San Francisco. Sometimes the entire family would come to the vineyard for a week's vacation so the children could all play. As the aunt's brother and wife got older, the children took over the store.

"I can say I am Maria and I was looking to get away for a bit." This time Luisa got up and started to follow him outside.

Giuseppe stopped, seemed to think for a moment and then turned towards her, "I don't know. I worry. This 'condition' as you call it, how do we know one day it will not all catch up to you. We know nothing of what really happened, although I feel there is more to it than what you told us. I don't want to take any chances. With papa gone now, I need to protect you and take care of you." He placed his hand on her cheek gently. "Besides, now might not be a good time to ask a family if they could feed another person. Luisa, times are hard right now, you know that." He rubbed his cheek with his thumb and forefinger thinking hard about this. "No, it's too much to ask." He proceeded to walk back outside; his decision was made.

"Giuseppe! You seem to forget who the parent is here! I have raised three fine children who do not need my assistance anymore. I love them with all my heart but I feel uncomfortable. If I was a little old woman, it would be different but I am not. I do not want to cause problems as the children get older and see that I am not aging."

Giuseppe stopped and turned. "Cause problems? Luisa...," he sighed. "Mama...you are never a problem. We love you so much." He stopped talking and shook his head. "But if this is something you want to do, how can I stop you? I will take you next week. We'll go to town to dial our cousin tomorrow and see what he thinks. Unfortunately, things have been quiet. It would be nice to see Angelo and his family."

She gave him a kiss and hug. "I will be back my love. Do not worry."

It just so happened that after Giuseppe called his cousin they were grateful of Luisa's visit. They could use help with the children since Angelo's wife had to help at the store more. They could not pay Luisa but she was grateful to help in any way she could.

The next week, Luisa spent time packing up some clothes to take. She didn't think she would need much. Although, she did hear that San Francisco had a lot going on. Luisa started to wonder if she should take advantage of this young body of hers that could still walk many miles and perhaps even dance, travel and see different places. She needed to get her mind off Lorenzo and how much she missed him. They told the family she was going on a long vacation but would return in less than a year. As Luisa gave everyone a hug and kiss goodbye, Giuseppe loaded the car with her belongings. It was such a great feeling for her to step back and look at them all, all of her children and grandchildren.

They had a long ride ahead of them. Luisa packed a small lunch for them both. Her son, Mario, was in charge of the vineyard while Giuseppe was away.

After about an hour Luisa started to get sleepy, the open valleys passing outside the window and the low hum of the engine lulled her to sleep.

1902

One evening after a day's work, I was washing up the children for dinner. They ran far ahead of me to the dining room. As I entered the room, there were a few men with Lorenzo and his cousins that I did not recognize. They were all laughing and drinking wine.

Lorenzo turned, saw me enter the room and put his arm toward me. "Here she is, my beautiful Luisa!" Lorenzo announced to the men.

"Luisa, this is Signore Alto and his two sons, Franco and Giovanni and Signore Alto's mother, Rosa. They used to work here years ago and had to leave due to a family matter. They are

13

here again to help us plant some new grape vines, a new varietal. Come here, say hello!"

I felt as if my legs would not move. It was *my* Giovanni. Almost fifteen years later and he looked better than I ever imagined. His hair was still dark brown and wavy only he had more mature features. He looked stronger now, although, the softness to his smile was still there, completely opposite of Lorenzo's rigid masculinity. I slowly walked towards them saying hello to each. I could see from the corner of my eye Giovanni kept looking down. It was so awkward when our eyes finally met. My hands were sweating and shaking as I lowered my head. Before I touched his hand to shake it gently, I wiped it on my dress hoping nobody noticed. So many years later, and I still felt nervous in his presence.

"Let's sit down for dinner," Lorenzo instructed. Everyone took a spot around the long table as I joined the other women in the kitchen to bring in the food.

Giovanni sat on the other side of the table opposite from where I was. His stare was burning through me. I wished he would stop, I was so nervous that Lorenzo would notice but thankfully he was too busy talking to the other men. It was a beautiful night outside. The doors were wide-open letting in the warm air. The glow of the candles on the table and the blue and orange sky from the sun setting was a perfectly relaxing scene.

But I could barely touch my meal and found myself constantly fidgeting with my fork or my drink and telling the children to settle down and eat. If only I could have done the same.

After dinner, all the men went to another room while the women cleaned up. Once the children had finished their milk, and all the dishes were cleaned, I decided to take the children outside for a little to run around on the patio before bed. I also needed the fresh air. So many thoughts were going through my head. Most of them were memories that I shared with Giovanni when I was younger.

It was so long ago, I hadn't thought of Giovanni much in all these years but now they were all running through my head again. It was all coming back so strongly and I was beginning to have mixed feelings.

I knew I loved Lorenzo. I loved what we had made as far as a family. Our beautiful children, delighting in the evening air. Everything was good. No, it was great. Why was I feeling like a young girl in love again? I felt so foolish. The other women were talking and laughing but I could not concentrate on what they were saying. Rosa, Giovanni's grandmother, was sitting in a chair crocheting lace, I stared at her for a moment. There was something very strange about her. She turned and caught my eye and I quickly looked away. She had a certain look in her eyes that spooked me, as if she knew what was going through my head. I got up and moved to the end of the court.

"Luisa, are you ok?" one of the other women asked.

"Yes, I must have drunk too much wine. I think I will retire for the evening."

I gathered my children and took them upstairs with me. As I passed the men on the way, I said goodnight without looking once at Giovanni.

That night Lorenzo came to bed in an exceptionally good mood. He loved new ideas for the business and seemed to have drunk a little too much himself. We made passionate love. It was wonderful. The only problem was during the entire time we made love, it was not him that I imagined being with. Not him at all. And I hated myself for it.

The next morning, after a sleepless night, I was almost frightened to walk in the kitchen for fear of seeing Giovanni. I had gotten up early and helped get coffee ready. My little one, Maria, was crying because she could not find her doll and forgot where she had left it. Fortunately for her, I remembered that she had left it in the other room. I reassured her I would go get it while she ate.

I started to walk in the sitting room and saw the doll on the floor next to the large chair where she had been playing the night before. I bent down to pick it up.

"Hello Luisa." It was Giovanni. I'd know that voice anywhere. I stood up suddenly and turned to face him, Maria's doll clenched tightly in my hands.

"Giovanni. It's good to see you."

He started to walk towards me smiling. I was nervous that someone would walk in the room.

"You look just as beautiful as you did when I left here."

"Thank you," I said extremely nervous. I do not even know how I managed to get those two words out.

"Luisa, I'm not sure if you were told what happened those many years ago. I do not want you to feel bad but your father spoke with mine about our relationship. The second he found out you were to marry Lorenzo he did not want to cause any problems with the Messina Family so we left to work on another vineyard. Just so you know, Lorenzo and his family have no idea what happened. You don't need to be worried that they will know the feelings I had for you, although I can say, they have never changed Luisa. I think of you all the time. I never met anyone like you."

I had no idea what to say in response. What did he expect? Why even say those things?

"I married too," he said softly. "It was for my family, like you. It was not for love, Luisa. You will always be my true love."

"Stop talking that way!" I snapped. I stalked past him as I hurried back towards the kitchen. My heart was pounding. Maria leapt off her chair, happy to see the doll in my hand.

"Thank you mama!" she cheered. I took comfort in her happiness and breathed deeply, thinking of Giovanni alone in the other room. How dare he say those things! I thought.

Days had passed and the men worked hard. I tried to avoid seeing Giovanni as much as I could, although I had no choice while we all ate. I admit that I did enjoy dinner more than ever. He made everyone laugh with his good humor.

16

One afternoon, I was outside cleaning the rugs watching the children play. Giovanni and his brother walked over and joined the children. They were having a great time and it was nice to see. Lorenzo was always so busy he did not have much time to play with them. In that moment it was as if Giovanni was a child himself. I didn't realize I had stopped what I was doing and started to watch them all instead, smiling the entire time. Before I knew it, Giovanni was walking towards me with an equally big smile and handed me a flower.

"For the prettiest lady."

"Giovanni, please…" I shook my head in disapproval and put the flower down on a table before someone saw.

"I didn't come here to cause you any problems. I just want to be your friend. Do you remember when we would laugh all the time? You understood me Luisa. I am not looking to take you away from this. I just miss your company, that's all."

"Mama look!" Mario yelled from a distance as he started to kick the ball around.

"That is wonderful my love!" I smiled back to him. My children were everything to me. I would not change it for anything in the world. Not even for Giovanni.

The next day, I was gathering some eggs out by the chicken cage when Giovanni came over to me.

"Can I help?" He did not come closer until I shook my head letting him know it was fine. I hesitated at first but then handed him a basket.

"How is your family doing?" he asked me, without looking but making sure to check each egg before he put it in the basket.

"They are well. My brother got his own vineyard and took my parents to live with them. It isn't too far from here. We visit with the children often."

I started to laugh and he looked at me.

"And what is so funny?" he said, wanting in on the joke.

"If my father knew you were here right now he would have a fit!"

He started to laugh also. "Yes, you are probably right about that one! He would not want me to ruin your life."

"He just wants what is best. But now he knows Lorenzo is taking care of me so he doesn't have much say anymore." I looked up at him. "What is your wife like?"

A big part of me was jealous that another woman was lucky enough to go to bed with him every night and wake up with him every morning. The most I ever got from Giovanni was a small kiss and hand-holding. I started to feel guilty for having such thoughts.

"She is a good woman. We have two children, a boy and a girl. I cannot complain, I guess. She doesn't understand me though. She doesn't laugh when I act silly in front of the kids. She takes everything serious and never relaxes. She does not understand when I draw either. She called it child's play and told me I should stop." He looked embarrassed to tell me.

"Oh Giovanni, I am sorry. I know how much you love drawing. Child's play? The best artists did their work as adults not children. That is silly. You were so good at your drawings. You should start again."

He laughed and sighed at the same time. "Ah, if only it were that easy. It's been a long time, I feel foolish."

"That's nonsense! It's a part of you; something you cannot ignore. I think you should start again Giovanni." I started to walk towards the house with the basket. Giovanni did not follow, which surprised me but also made me happy, I did not want anyone to see us together. Maybe he was thinking about drawing again.

Chapter 4

They must have hit a bump on the way because Luisa was jolted awake.

"Oh, I'm sorry, Luisa!" Giuseppe looked at her with a worried face. "You were having a nice sleep."

"It's ok," she told him, as she started to sit up. "Are you getting hungry yet?" She looked to the back at the basket she packed.

"Yes, let's eat, that sounds good." He pulled over to the side of the road. There was an open area and they decided to put a blanket down and eat. He needed a break from driving anyway.

Luisa handed him bread and cheese with some meat on the side. They both drank water along with grapes and cookies after. Giuseppe had some wine in the back that was supposed to be for Cousin Angelo but they had some of it anyway. Luisa felt happy to sit with her son who looked more like her older brother. She was proud of how confident and strong he had become. To think that she once almost threw all of it away and might not have been around for them amazes her.

"Mama…" He looked at her hesitantly. She knew he was being serious when he called her that. "What really happened to you? I can't explain it but you must know something, a family secret maybe? What has made you stay young? It's just so incredible."

She looked at him and then turned away towards the beautiful scenery. She decided that it was time he knew just as much as she did. He was old enough to handle the truth about what happened that night. Luisa still could not explain what happened to her but she could explain as much as she could to her son. She hoped he would not judge her. Although, she wasn't sure how he would take the truth.

Looking at him, she smiled and said, "I worry because I don't want you to think any differently of me. I am not happy with my choices that night, but you must know, in the end, I did nothing wrong. You'll understand what I mean after I tell you."

He didn't say a word, just shook his head in agreement. Luisa then proceeded to tell him what he has always wanted to know.

19

1902

Giovanni and his family had been staying with us for close to two weeks now. We were all getting used to the company. Their grandmother, Rosa, was helpful with the children and cooking. She insisted on helping all the time. I would sometimes catch her staring at me from across the room, smiling.

One afternoon I walked out to tell the children to come inside and get washed up. I saw Giovanni sitting at the table with Maria. They were drawing something. Maria saw me come out and showed me her drawing.

"Look mama! I drew a bird! Gio is teaching me, isn't it beautiful?" She held up the paper for me to see. It really was a pretty picture.

"I hope you don't mind. I saw her drawing and I couldn't help but sit with her." He looked at me hopeful I would not be upset.

"Of course not, thank you, that was sweet to do," I said to him as I turned to Maria. "Maria, Giovanni is busy, you cannot keep him from his work for too long."

"Oh it's no trouble," he said.

Maria ran off with her picture excited to show all the other children what she had drawn. It was just Giovanni and I alone. I wasn't as nervous as I used to be near him, I felt very comfortable with him actually.

"I would like to start drawing again...while I am here at least. Do you think you can take a walk with me? Just to find something beautiful that could inspire me."

Now I was nervous again. I would love to take a walk with him just as we used to. Although, I knew it would not be the right thing to do, it had been a long morning and I was getting tired of kneading dough and cleaning. A walk would be a relief. I took off my apron, wiping my hands. "Ok, just for a little." I started to walk as Giovanni collected Maria's paper and utensils, and followed.

****

Lorenzo and his cousin Franco were out in the vineyard that day too. Franco had moved from the family vineyard in Sicily to work with Lorenzo in California. They grew up together on the vineyard and Franco was Lorenzo's closest friend.

He said that Franco told him he was surprised that Lorenzo was ok working with the Alto family after what happened. When Lorenzo questioned him, Franco realized he was not aware of what happened those many years ago. Of course, Franco was sorry he brought it up but Lorenzo insisted he tell him. He told Lorenzo that Senior Alto found out his son, Giovanni and I were getting close with one another. He then packed up leaving the vineyard so as not to cause any trouble. He knew that Lorenzo and I were to wed one day.

Lorenzo did not show it to Franco but he was very upset upon hearing this. We met at such a young age he never imagined another man could have gotten between us. As confident as he was about our relationship, of course he felt jealous as well as foolish for even entertaining this man in our home.

Giovanni and I started to walk into the meadow. From there you could not see the house, which in a way, was a good thing. As we walked, I had to wonder if Giovanni chose this way because of how quickly you were out of view from the house. The hill went up and once you passed it you went over the hill and down into an open area that was blocked off from the house and vineyards by trees. At first, I was a bit nervous about this but at the same time relieved. No one would know, or see the smile on my face as we wandered together.

"What makes you happy, Luisa?" Giovanni asked me with a smile. Goosebumps exploded all over my arms when he looked at me.

"What makes me happy?" Nobody ever asked what made me happy before. It was just expected of me to be a mother and a wife. To do what was needed and that was it.

21

Lorenzo never asked me anything like that. My life with Lorenzo was almost like a job. We did have our moments of intimacy but it was never about my feelings and if I was happy with where my life was.

"I suppose my children of course," I answered.

"Ok, yes, they are wonderful children. But aside from them, what do you enjoy?" He wasn't letting me get away with such an easy answer.

"I don't know! What do you mean? Food! Food makes me happy ok?" I shook my head laughing, knowing very well this was not the kind of answer he was looking for. However, I didn't have time for hobbies or interest. I had to take care of things around the house and with my family. I wasn't sure what made me happy, aside from the children.

Giovanni stopped walking and looked around into the trees. He then put his hand out and motioned for me to have a seat in the grass.

"Close your eyes. Do not think of what you need to do back at the house. Just relax. You have the day all to yourself. What would you do? What do you feel, Luisa?" He slowly took my hand and caressed my fingers. His hand was not as rough as Lorenzo's was. He was so gentle. Smooth.

The trees rustled as their leaves brushed against each other from the wind. I heard some birds chirping as they flew overhead and felt the sun shining down on my face. It was then when I realized what made me happy but I could not say that to him. I was happy to be there with him enjoying the moment. Just talking and laughing. I told him how I felt free. How I would love to enjoy the day lying in the sun with the breeze on my face.

"Keep your eyes closed. Tell me what you hear."

I continued to answer all of his questions. The more we talked the more relaxed I found myself. He then told me to open my eyes. Giovanni was holding up the pad he brought with him so that I could see what he drew as my eyes were closed. It was a picture of me relaxing with trees and hills surrounding me.

"Oh my goodness, that is amazing."

"Yes, she is."

"I need to get back." I quickly got up and started to walk towards the house.

"Luisa! I am sorry if I made you uncomfortable. I just miss you and I have never met anyone so wonderful. I wish I never left you, but I had no choice." Giovanni was walking fast trying to catch up to me. "I was too young to make my own decisions. I hope you know that. If I could go back I – "

I cut him off. "No, please do not say any of this to me. I have a life now with Lorenzo. I have children. Things are different now. They have to be."

I continued to walk and he continued to keep up. That only made me more nervous. I wished he had stopped and stayed behind.

As I neared the house, Lorenzo was outside waiting for me. I stopped and looked at him, almost frightened, even guilty. He smiled and started to walk towards me until he saw Giovanni running up behind me. Giovanni also stopped when he saw Lorenzo.

"Where were you Luisa?" Lorenzo asked me.

Giovanni interrupted, "I asked her to help me with something Lorenzo. I apologize for keeping her."

I continued to walk towards the house, right past Lorenzo.

Later that evening after dinner was cleaned up and all the children were in bed I walked into our bedroom.

"How was your walk today?" Lorenzo asked me as he put his clothes away, facing away from me.

"Oh Lorenzo, please do not question me the way you are. I simply went for a walk with Giovanni to show him quiet places where he could do some drawings. He wanted to draw a nature scene. I worked hard all day and did not see it a big deal to take a walk."

"Drawing? What man draws?" he snorted as if to make Giovanni look foolish.

23

I climbed into bed next to him and gave him a kiss on the cheek. "You are the only man I see, the only one."

Days went on and Giovanni and I kept our distance. He did not socialize with the children either, even though they tried to always get him to kick the ball around or draw. He would make an excuse that he was too busy at the moment. I knew it was better to be safe and not be caught talking with him but I had to admit, I now longed for Giovanni's company and attention. He would not even look me in the eyes during any of the meals.

That night at dinner, Lorenzo lifted his wine and announced that the Alto family's work was complete and that they will be leaving in the morning. He thanked them for their hard work and looked forward to working with them again one day. After hearing this, I felt such mixed emotions. Relief that I could go on the way it was, not worrying about anyone seeing me speak with Giovanni, but at the same time, I felt heartbroken that this could be the last time I see him. He was leaving me again. My body felt lifeless and I had pains inside of me that I didn't even know could exist.

We all raised our glasses wishing the family well. Giovanni and I looked at each other longer than we should have and I hoped that nobody noticed.

Later that evening after the children were in bed, I went outside for some fresh air. Most of the men were still gathering in the main room laughing and drinking, enjoying their last evening together. I went out back without telling anyone so I could be alone. I decided to go out to the barn where the horses were. It always seemed to relax me when I would brush the horses. I lit a couple of the lanterns and brought them with me as guidance through the dark. When I got inside, I placed one on each side so that I could see most of the room.

Bella was my favorite horse. She was older than the other horses but was the calmest. She nickered at me and I pressed my face to hers, breathing in the smell of warm hay.

"You are beautiful, Bella," I told her as I brushed her hair.

"So are you Luisa." I was startled and whirled around. Giovanni was standing in the doorway watching me.

"Giovanni, it's not a good idea to be here alone with each other. Lorenzo seemed to act funny the day he saw us come back from our walk." I placed the brush back on the wall and proceeded to walk past him to leave. He grabbed my arm gently. His touch alone made me shiver.

"Luisa I don't want to leave without saying goodbye to you. I wish I could stay longer."

"Giovanni, I wish you the best in your life. I really must get back." I left the barn and headed back towards the kitchen holding in tears. It occurred to me at that moment that I left the lanterns in the barn and I know Lorenzo would be very upset if he knew I did that. I could not go back if Giovanni was there. I decided to go around the back of the barn so that he couldn't see me. It was dark enough outside that he would not notice if I went around to the side of the barn instead of straight across.

As I went through the side door, I could hear two men talking. Their voices rising in volume. "Nothing is going on!" Giovanni yelled.

The next thing I heard was Lorenzo's voice. "I see how you look at her!"

My stomach dropped as I imagined he must have seen me in there with Giovanni just moments ago. I got closer to hear better. My hands were shaking as I moved to the other side of the barn to get a better view. I moved as quietly as I could and hid behind the haystacks.

"I know why your family left many years ago Giovanni. My cousin was kind enough to inform me the other day. I don't want any trouble with your father but I will do what I need to in order to keep you away from my wife! How dare you take her out to the meadow for a walk alone! Did you think I did not notice that you followed her out here as well, at night while she was alone?" I never heard Lorenzo yell the way he did that night.

"Lorenzo, I am sorry, I do not dare to disrespect you or your family. Luisa and I were just friends those many years ago.

25

We were children. It was just nice to spend time with her that's all."

I could not believe what I heard him say next.

"Lorenzo, I hope you know what a wonderful wife you have. I do regret not being the one to marry her myself. I know she would've have been happy with me."

I don't know why he said that to Lorenzo. *Why couldn't he just let it go?* I covered my mouth with my hands in shock not knowing how Lorenzo would take such disrespect.

"I should throw you out with my bare hands right now for saying that!"

The next thing I knew I heard Bella going wild and objects crashing against the floor and walls. They must have started to fight. If I ran out there then Lorenzo would think I was in there hiding with Giovanni. I was hoping someone from the house would hear this and come out to stop them. Suddenly, there was a bright light in front of me. It took me by surprise, which then caused me to fall back. They were flames. One of the lanterns knocked over and had fallen in the hay. The fire went all the way to the side door that I entered on. I could see the look on Lorenzo's face; he was shocked at what he had done. Giovanni yelled Lorenzo's name and dragged him out. "Come on Lorenzo! Let's get out of here!"

They both ran taking the two horses with them. Unfortunately, I was still inside. I couldn't go back the way I entered so I ran for where the men were first standing. I could now hear more voices yelling outside. They were probably trying to take the fire out. I started to scream but I don't think anyone heard me. It was then that I heard very faintly Lorenzo's voice, "Luisa?" He must have heard me.

I kept yelling to make sure he did hear me. I was looking for any way out but the fire had spread so fast it seemed hopeless. I grabbed one of the blankets and covered myself in it looking for a place to run. Something fell into me. I thought I was seeing things. It was Giovanni.

"Come with me Luisa, I broke through over there!" He pulled me towards that direction. I could hear the wood breaking and falling all around us. There seemed to be nowhere to go! Giovanni held me close and was practically carrying me across the barn to the opening that he made. We had to climb over barrels and boxes that were everywhere and it was so difficult to see in front of us with all the smoke and flames. Above us, you could see that the fire moved up to the loft. We were almost there; I could see the small opening. Suddenly there was an extremely loud bang. The top of the loft fell right in front of us. Giovanni reacted quickly by covering me with the blanket and pushing me down to the floor. I could see then that a log of wood hit him in the head as he fell to the floor. I felt so weak and knew I could never make it out alone. My children were all I could think about at that moment. I would do anything to see them again and couldn't bear the thought of them losing their mother. I became upset with myself and managed to yell Giovanni's name but he wouldn't budge.

I sat there with him crying and screaming as I hit him to get up. I couldn't breathe anymore. Everything that happened after that was blank in my mind.

Chapter 5

Luisa stopped talking and looked over at her son. She was happy to see that he was not looking at her with disapproval in his eyes. Instead, he seemed more sympathetic.

"I never knew this tragedy happened to you both. I do remember the fire in the barn, I just did not know that's how it happened. Our lives always seemed so simple. I would never imagine something so dramatic would have happened to you and pop." Giovanni paused shaking his head in disbelief. "Well, you are here so it must have turned out fine right? What was the next thing you remembered?"

****

All I could remember next was waking up screaming.

"Ok Luisa, its ok!" It was Lorenzo. He was sitting on the bed next to me. "It's me my love. You are ok. You are here with me. Look…the children are here too!"

I looked over and saw my children, all three of them crying. They looked so frightened.

Suddenly it all was coming back to me. The last thing I remembered was being in the barn. All I could think of is that I must have been burned in the fire. Badly. So much that I must be scaring the children.

"Lorenzo! Take them out of here; do not let them see me like this!" I managed to yell. I did not want my children to be so upset seeing their mother horribly disfigured, although I felt no pain I was sure that I had been burnt all over.

"Its ok Luisa, they are tears of joy. They are as happy as I am to see you!" Lorenzo had tears streaming down his cheeks and his bottom lip was quivering.

I heard another voice then. "She needs her rest now." I could see it was my sister-in-law, Pina. She had a rag and asked

28

everyone to leave so that I could get some rest. She took the rag and wiped my forehead down. The coldness of it was a relief.

"I will be back a little later. Get some rest ok?" Lorenzo took the kids and left the room.

Pina came and sat down next to me. "You gave us all a scare there, Luisa."

"What happened? How did I get out of the barn?"

"All the men broke through and carried you and Giovanni out."

"Giovanni? Is he alright?" Pina was not answering, instead she kept looking at the rag in her hand. "Pina, answer me? Is Giovanni ok?" I looked worried and then I saw her face turn into anger.

"Giovanni did not make it Luisa! They took his body home right after the fire. Nobody knows what happened. Lorenzo will not talk to anyone. He blames himself for everything that happened. What were you two doing in that barn, Luisa?"

I stopped listening to her. My head fell back down on the pillow. I just looked up at the ceiling. I couldn't even manage tears. I was in too much shock. Giovanni died because of me. Meanwhile, Lorenzo was taking blame for it. None of this should have happened.

"Please leave me be right now, Pina." She stopped talking and left the room, grimacing.

The next few days I stayed in bed. I had no desire to eat anything. I managed to have some bread and noticed that I started to feel great, physically but not emotionally. The children would spend time with me and make me smile, but it was so hard to fake it. I did not want to smile or eat. In fact, I had no desire to do anything. I was in a separate room by myself. That is where I stayed. It was only a week and I was still feeling the guilt of Giovanni's death. The dread of what his family must be thinking of me, especially his wife. I wished they never came in the first place.

After a while, I started to do work around the house again. Things were getting back to normal. The workers were

29

building up the barn. There were moments I would look out of the window into the meadow as I was cleaning the dishes and remember the walk I had with Giovanni that day. How he told me his true feelings.

Things with Lorenzo were different, too. He seemed to pay more attention to me. He never asked me what I was doing in the barn that night with Giovanni. Instead, one night, to alleviate any doubt he may have, I told him up front.

I joined him in bed and looked at him with concern.

"Lorenzo, I think we should talk about what happened that night. I don't feel right inside thinking you are having these terrible thoughts about me."

He put his hand up as if to silence me. "Luisa, please. I saw you. I have been watching ever since Franco let me know what happened those many years ago." He laughed and shook his head in disappointment. "I should have never questioned our love for each other Luisa." Looking up at me he looked into my eyes. "I hope you can forgive me for ever doubting what we have. I blame myself for everything that happened that night. I saw you leave once you saw Giovanni come to the barn. I didn't trust him. You are so beautiful, of course he still had feelings for you. However, no longer will we discuss his feelings for you again. No matter how I might have felt about Giovanni, I will not disrespect him or his family. We will not speak of the dead that way. Let's be happy we were so lucky and my foolishness did not cost us your life, too. I love you so much Luisa. I hope I am the man you always wished me to be."

Without hesitation, I placed my head on his chest. "Lorenzo I love you so much. None of this is your fault at all. Please know that."

That night we slept in each other's arms.

The next evening Lorenzo and I decided to sit outside and enjoy the warm night after the children were all in bed.

"I have something to speak with you about." He pulled out a letter from his pocket and opened it up.

"It turns out, my uncle who lives in America," he said, paused and looked up at me momentarily before looking back down at the letter in his hand. "California exactly, is asking me if I want an opportunity to be partners with him." He seemed nervous telling me about this.

"Oh, is he planning to buy a vineyard in Sicily?" I looked at him trying to picture us living in another home. I never lived anywhere else except here. I was nervous to hear his answer, knowing his uncle would not be purchasing land in Sicily.

Maybe a move would be a nice change, I thought. *Especially if it would only be us living on the property.* I was starting to get annoyed with all the whispering going on lately with the other women, it would be nice to escape them.

"Actually, in America." He paused and continued to look at the letter, before lifting his wonder-filled eyes to my face.

"What? Lorenzo! Leave Sicily? How could we? The children, our family! Just leave it all?" I got up waving my hands around. It was a terrifying thought now that he said it out loud. I couldn't believe he even considered reading this to me. Why didn't he throw the letter away or at least write him that we could not possibly do this?

"I just thought, maybe…I don't know. We could start new. America is full of opportunities. I would be doing something I know so well. You think about it. I will answer him when we are ready." Lorenzo got up and went inside, taking the note with him. Before the fire, I wouldn't have much of a say in this if it were something Lorenzo wanted to do. Lately, he was more conscious of my own feelings. The first thing that came to my head was the years when I first started to talk to Lorenzo. He told me how he one day hoped to go to America and bring me with him. This was a dream of his and who was I to ruin it?

That night in bed, my head started to hurt. I sat up holding the back of my head.

"What is it?" Lorenzo asked, waking out of a sleep.

"It's just my head. It feels funny."

31

"Signora Alto said that you might experience some pains here and there. She kept telling me that things would be different with you from now on and that I need to accept it. I guess the headaches are part of this change! Who knows? That lady was very strange."

"How would she know how I would feel? And what do you mean by *change*?"

At this question, Lorenzo sighed. He sat up held my hand and proceeded to tell me exactly what happened the night of the fire.

"We managed to break open the hole in the back of the barn more. A few of us went inside. Others tried to put it out. I saw you lying on the floor. Luisa, I thought you were dead." Lorenzo stopped talking and looked down at his hands. "I dragged you out and we tried everything we could. I picked you up in my arms and carried you to the house. It was so terrible. Pina took the children away so they didn't see you like that. There was no movement; you laid there on the couch as I sat next to you crying. It was then that Signora Alto came in and stood over you. She told me to leave and that she would take care of you. I tried to tell her through tears it was too late. She yelled for me to leave before it truly was. My brother pulled me away." Lorenzo stopped talking, holding back tears. Then he managed to continue. "I left her with you, I was so confused and so upset. I felt lost. So much had been ruined and so quickly. The only woman I could ever love was gone. It was my entire fault. I waited in the kitchen for what seemed like an eternity. Then, she came out, calm as a summer day. She told us to put you in a room where you could rest. I didn't understand this, I thought you were gone, Luisa. As far as Giovanni, she was with him first. Signora Alto said it was too late for him."

At hearing this, I cried. Lorenzo mentioning Giovanni's death was a terrible reminder of what I lost. Lorenzo was not upset at my crying.

"The Alto family went home immediately to bring Giovanni's body to his family. Right before they left, Signora said to me that things would be different for you now. That your body will remain the way it is for a very long time and that she could not explain further. She said you would remain the same age always. I dismissed what she said, still do. The woman is crazy as I said. She kept asking if I understood. I told her yes not really knowing what it was I understood. I supposed she just meant that you would always remain young at heart. Who knows?"

Chapter 6

Giuseppe's face was astonished. He looked at his mother confused.

"So, you are telling me that this old woman did something to you that made your body remain young? Impossible!"

Luisa laughed. "Impossible eh? Look at me Giuseppe! I don't know how she did it but she did something. She saved my life. Without her, I wouldn't have been there for our family all those years. Your father said I was hardly breathing after they pulled me out of that barn. How do you explain that?"

Giuseppe got up and started to pace back and forth with his arms crossed. He tried to come up with some sort of explanation but couldn't. He then laughed and said, "I don't know. I just don't know but you are right. You are proof! What more can I say?"

Giuseppe had so many more questions, and Luisa tried her best to answer them. "What if something else were to happen to you again? Like the fire? Worse? Would you still…die?"

"I don't know. Your father and I wondered the same thing. Of course, we never tried to test it but I can tell you that there were many times that I hurt myself by accident and it seemed to heal instantly."

At that moment, Luisa hesitated and took the small paring knife she had in the basket. Giuseppe lunged towards her. "No Luisa! We don't need to take a chance! Put it down!"

Luisa hid the knife behind her back and put her other hand on his shoulder. "It's ok."

She backed up and took the edge of the knife to her hand and gently pierced her palm until she drew blood. She winced a bit but then, right in front of their eyes the cut started to close.

Giuseppe got up and stepped back holding his head. "What? This can't be good! So what does this mean? You will walk the earth forever?"

"Believe me, as time goes by I am learning that this is a curse, not a blessing. At first, it was wonderful. All the happy times I had after the accident, I realized there was a chance I would never have been there to see my children. However, here you all are, much older, still growing and successful. Oh Giuseppe, I don't know what to make of this anymore. To keep hiding all the time is getting tiring. Your father always told me I need to keep this to myself or perhaps doctors would take me and try to experiment on me. Who knows?"

"Yes, yes we must keep you safe. I will do that mama. But tell me, when did you realize that you were not aging?"

It started with the instant healing.

****

After our move to America, I was preparing dinner one night, cutting up carrots on the wooden board. Somehow, I managed to cut the edge of my thumb. My instant reaction was like anyone else's. I dropped everything and headed over to the sink to rinse the blood that started to appear, but by the time I got to the sink the cut was gone. I rinsed the blood off, but there was no cut beneath. I couldn't understand it. I told Lorenzo about it that night and he just suggested that I probably didn't cut myself as bad as I had thought I did. I thought perhaps he was right, that I must have imagined cutting myself that badly. But there was no mark at all to explain the blood.

I was doing a lot of cooking, so this happened a couple more times. All of the women's hands had marks on them from something. However, each time I got cut or burned it healed instantly. Lorenzo didn't say much when I would tell him. He would just tell me not to worry and not to tell anyone because of what they would think.

So the years went by and it wasn't obvious at all that I hadn't aged. There are always people who always look young. That's just good genes, they would say.

I never thought anything about it, until a few years later. Lorenzo and I were talking and I brought up how all the other women were telling me how lucky I was that I hadn't gotten any wrinkles yet or grey hair. They wanted to know how I did it, how I had been so lucky.

It was those moments, where the women were complaining about their looks, that Lorenzo would remind me of what Signora Alto said the night of the fire. Between her words,

35

and my instant healing, things weren't right. We agreed to accept whatever it was and over time see what happens.

One year, Lorenzo's brother and family came from Sicily to visit us.

After dinner my sister-in-law Pina and I were sitting outside relaxing.

"Do you still think of him?" she asked.

I looked over at her confused. "Who?"

"You know, Giovanni." She didn't look at me, just forward.

I shook my head. "Pina, stop." Truth was, I thought of Giovanni all the time. I felt so responsible for his death. It bothered me that his poor wife and children had lost him. They lost their father all because of me. I wondered if Pina thought the same and disrespected me for that. I would never have talked to her about him in the past but tonight seemed to be different.

"Luisa, I don't judge you. You and I didn't marry for love. You know, there was a boy that I had a crush on when I was younger. I wished that I would have been able to marry him instead. Don't get me wrong, I love my life now. It's just, I couldn't imagine how great life would be to be able to marry someone who you loved. We all know how you and Giovanni were close many years ago. It's ok Luisa. I felt bad for you. Not at first though. I admit at first I was angry with you. I felt bad for Lorenzo. But I know you did nothing wrong. You are a good wife and a good mother. But from one woman to another, I want you to know I understand." She placed her hand on mine and squeezed it. It was the closest I had ever felt to her and I really appreciated it.

I figured I owed her some sort of answer. "Yes, I think of him. Sometimes, that is. I think of his family. I wish things were different for them. It didn't seem fair the way it all turned out."

She looked over at me. "You know it really was a strange time. I was there when Lorenzo took you into the living room and placed you on the couch. You were so close to dying yourself. You really should be happy to have survived. Don't feel bad. I remember the following days, being so confused. The night of the fire you had cuts and burns all over your face and arms. Somehow, the next day they were all gone. I was the one cleaning you up and taking care of you. It was as if one minute they were there and the next minute they were gone. I mean, I literally got up to go wash the rag out in the sink to clean up the cuts and when I got back and wiped your face...it's like it was just dirt." She continued to look at me as if perhaps I knew the answer but I didn't. If anything I was concerned, both about her knowledge and about what Signora Alto had done to me.

When I told Lorenzo what she had said he nodded and gripped my hand the same way Pina had earlier that afternoon. Signora Alto, Rosa, had told Lorenzo that I would never age. That I would remain the same age for a very long time.

It was then that we started to believe. I didn't look a day older than that night of the fire. We didn't know what happened or what she did. It was all so confusing. We believed in God, so of course we thought perhaps she was an angel and performed a miracle of some sorts. But another part of us wondered the exact opposite. This could be the work of witchcraft. Only God can control these things. It made me crazy.

Lorenzo and I promised that we would attribute this miracle to God. It had to be.

Of course, there were nights when I would think it couldn't be and I was being punished for my actions with Giovanni. Even though I did no wrong, I certainly had thoughts about doing something wrong.

****

It started getting late and Giuseppe knew they had to continue on their way. After a long ride, they made it to their Cousin Angelo's house. It was a wonderful visit and as Giuseppe left, he gave his mother a hug and kiss wishing her well. He let her know that he will be back to get her whenever she was ready.

Luisa ended up living with them for a few years. During this time, she would frequently go back and forth to see her own family. She missed the grandchildren and at times wished she could play the role of grandmother but it just wasn't possible. She enjoyed her stay at

37

Angelo's and helped in the store and with the family. They were very protective of Luisa. Many men would approach her asking if they could get to know her more but she was not ready for anything like that. She enjoyed her time there and would go out on occasion with some new friends she made. It was very different from living on a vineyard. This was more exciting but she saw a lot of hardship as well. So many people were out of work. Luisa helped as much as she could within the community. Life on the vineyard was hard but not as bad as what she witnessed there. On the vineyard, there weren't just grapes growing. Lorenzo had made sure to grow enough crops that the whole family could survive. They also had a farm with chickens and pigs in which they managed as well. Giuseppe also tried his hardest to keep as many staff as possible.

Luisa did meet a man during her stay in San Francisco. He was a friend of the family that she enjoyed spending time with on occasion. Everyone would get together as a group and during these times she would spend time with him. He made her laugh always and was very handsome. They had gotten to know each other very well and when he wanted to make their relationship more serious she backed away. It was then that Luisa decided to move back to the vineyard.

Chapter 7

Luisa's days on the vineyard were long. The years seemed to pass slowly. What upset Luisa the most was watching everyone get older except for her. She would dream about growing old with Lorenzo. Being grandparents and sitting back in the chairs watching the little ones play while the older children took care of the work. Instead, she saw her own children grow older and become grandparents themselves.

After many years, she moved to a family friend's house in which she stayed for over ten years. The woman's husband had died and the woman lived alone. She never had any children so Luisa agreed to help her out. Giuseppe saw it as an opportunity to hide her for a bit so that the children did not question her youth. In addition, he figured Luisa could use the change. When the woman passed away, she returned to the vineyard. As happy as she was to see the family it seemed to be a dead end in her life. They told the grandchildren that Luisa was a cousin of the family. It was then she had to try to look on the younger side and she cut her hair rather short. It was too much for her to take, all the lies and hiding. Nevertheless, the years passed. Her grandchildren had children of their own. Her daughter, Maria, lived with her husband not too far away. Mario lived on the vineyard with his family along with Luisa and Giuseppe. Over the years, Luisa would live with Maria for a change and stay to help her with all the children. It was nice to watch them all grow but again, Luisa felt lost most of the time.

Nobody seemed to question about Luisa any longer. They just accepted it and knew it was never to be spoken of. Luisa grew close to her great grandchildren. They were of a different time. More lively, more ambitious than when she was a young girl. They were fun to be with and Luisa enjoyed having many conversations with them. It was the one thing that made her happy and the one thing that helped her get through her days. They all helped her learn English. At this point Luisa was fluent. There were only so many things for her to do to keep her busy throughout the day. Luisa often wondered, what would she do when they grew old themselves?

There were so many lonely times for her and she wished for the company of Lorenzo. It seemed so long ago that he was once with her on this earth. Many times, she prayed for her own death. She knew that day might never come.

As she watched her children getting older and sicker, the pain was too much for her. She spoke to Giuseppe about this, begging him to help her do something to end all the pain.

"I can't. I can't sit back anymore and watch this! Please, help me Giuseppe. I can't do this myself. I need you to do something."

Giuseppe was much older, in his seventies. Forty years has passed since Luisa told him the entire story. He would see her wandering the vineyards, stressed. He understood what she was asking of him but couldn't possibly help her. He no longer saw her as his mother. So many years had passed that she was like his daughter now. He could never harm her, not in any way, even if he wanted to.

One night he heard screaming coming from her bedroom. Horrible, gut-wrenching cries, followed by the crash of a dish breaking. He ran to her room letting everyone know he would take care of it. He opened the door with caution not knowing what he would find.

"Luisa? Luisa what's the matter? Luisa!" She was on the floor, her knees hugged to her chest, sobbing. Giuseppe sat on the bed beside her and put his hand on her shoulder. He saw the cup broken on the floor across the room.

"I can't even die! No matter what I do it just won't work!"

"What have you done?" Giuseppe demanded. She pursed her lips and refused to respond. He didn't see any blood but looked up at the table next to her bed. There was a box of poison used to keep the rodents away. Luisa had poured it into her coffee, and over an hour later: nothing. Nothing happened to her. She hadn't even felt sick. The worst was a tickle in her stomach, and she wasn't even sure it was from the poison.

It was then Giuseppe knew he needed to give her a purpose in life. More than what she has right now. He thought of his children. Times were changing and his grandson Michael wanted to do more in his life than work with wine on a vineyard. He wanted to be a journalist and write for newspapers. Not just any newspaper though. All he ever talked about was to work in New York City. Giuseppe didn't like him speaking about it and would always yell at him to stop talking nonsense when there was work to be done. It twisted his gut to yell at his grandson, but dreams rarely came true.

He saw that his grandson was happiest when writing stories. The way he would always ask a thousand and one questions whenever there was something going on. The way he would detail each moment in his journal, analyzing the facts. Out of all the grandchildren, they managed to send Michael to a local college. They figured he had enough ambition and his grades were high so why not give him what he wanted? Everyone else stayed in the family business and worked on the vineyard. Giuseppe first thought it was a bad idea. But his grandson's happiness could never be a bad idea to him, and so Giuseppe had an idea to save his mother.

"Luisa. What do you think about taking Michael to New York City? He would have his great grandmother there for protection. Perhaps you can start a new life there as well?"

Luisa slowly stopped crying and looked up at Giuseppe. She didn't move or say anything. He let her sit and think this through with no further mention, got up and walked out of the room.

Chapter 8

1974

Giuseppe's friend, Francesco, and his family, had moved to a subsection of New York City, called Queens. Francesco started a business that turned out to be successful enough and the family chose to stay there permanently. Giuseppe phoned him that week telling his friend of the plan and asked if he could help in any way.

"It just so happens, that there is a very small apartment available for them to rent in our building," Francesco said. So a few months of saving would let Giuseppe send Luisa and Michael to New York. Francesco even found a job for Luisa sewing at the local tailor.

One night, after dinner was finished, some of the women started to get up to clear the table.

"If everyone could please sit back down for a second, there is something I would like to say," Giuseppe said to them, motioning his hands for them to sit back down. It was remarkable for Luisa to see that her son had become elderly.

"You might not understand what it is I am going to explain to you. In fact, I cannot even explain it. However, I can say, that with my own eyes, I have experienced something that I have no answer to. You all maybe be wondering what family it is that Luisa comes from. I have told most of you that she is a cousin of ours. However, I never gave more information than that. I appreciate your silence with the matter. Some of you were told something that you probably do not believe." He looked over at his wife.

Giuseppe slowly got up from his chair. He was not as quick and strong as he used to be. He walked over to where Luisa was sitting and put his hands on her shoulders and slowly looked around the table.

"Luisa is my mother."

Nobody said a word but they all looked at each other in confusion. Mario looked directly at his glass of wine. He was getting tired of people asking him about Luisa and he never knew what to say. All this time he didn't believe it to be true himself and waited all these years for Luisa, his own mother, to age. It never happened. It just became a normal part of life for him.

Michael, Giuseppe's grandson asked, "What are you talking about nonno? I think that would be a little impossible!" He chuckled,

42

which gave everyone else a sign that it was safe for them to laugh as well.

Giuseppe moved over to a buffet table on the other side of the room and opened up a drawer with a key he had in his pocket. In there, he pulled out some pictures and bought them over to the table. He handed them out for everyone to look at.

"As you can see, these are pictures of me when I was much younger. You all know it's me in the picture, yes? Look there, next to me. That is Luisa. Now, look at her right here at this table. You see the same woman there in that picture. Now, look at this picture."

He handed out another one. Lorenzo had taken a picture of the family when their children were young.

"In that picture I am about 12 years old. Look at my parents. Look at my mother. Now, I ask you, look here." He was now standing behind Luisa and put his hands back on her shoulder. "Look at my mother."

Luisa finally looked up at everyone with a serious face on.

Everyone started to talk now. All at once saying how impossible it was, yelling over each other. Giuseppe held up a wrinkled hand and the room fell silent. He explained to them that they did not know how it had happened, nor why – only that it had. He said there was an accident and an old woman, a friend of the family, was alone with her for a little. After that, ever since that night, Luisa remained young forever.

"This must be kept between our families. Nobody would believe you anyway. It's our duty to keep Luisa safe. Away from people who might want to test her. As you may know, life has been very hard on Luisa. Watching loved ones grow old. Some of them have died. Well, Luisa needs a change, a big change. I decided, I think it best if Luisa traveled to New York City."

Hearing those words, Michael moved forward in his chair. Just hearing New York City caused excitement for him. Moreover, when he saw his grandfather look directly at him, his stomach dropped, not knowing what words would come next.

Giuseppe smiled and laughed, seeing the excitement already on Michael's face. "Yes, Michael. I would like you to accompany my mother to New York. I think she can protect you just as much as you can protect her. You will both be on the train this Thursday. I already discussed this with your parents. It's time for our family to spread out and have more opportunities."

Some of the other grandchildren seemed to be jealous, but Michael was the oldest, and most suited to travel, and it made sense to send him. Michael got up and gave his grandfather a hug and kiss. Then he went over to his parents. His mother was holding back tears, "I know you will make us proud," was all she could manage to say. He kissed her gently on the forehead. Then he ran to his room to start packing.

Giuseppe saw them off to the train station that week. He gave Luisa a long hug and whispered in her ear, "I know you will take care of your great grandson. Go, start a new life." At that, he smiled gently and gave his grandson a hug. They both stepped on the train filled with excitement.

The train ride was a long one. Michael was curious to hear all about Luisa's story. She told about the fire, but Luisa did not mention Giovanni at all. After their talk, she looked over at him. "You should get some sleep Michael, we have a lot to do once we arrive." She took his hand in hers. "It's you and me now. We're a team right? You need to stay out of trouble; we can't let your grandpa down."

Michael smiled at her tightening his hand around hers. "Don't worry Luisa, I mean nonna. Well what should I call you now?"

She laughed. "Luisa is just fine. Remember, I am your older sister once we arrive in New York."

"Ok sis!" They both laughed.

Michael settled back, and slowly drifted off to sleep. Luisa stared out the window, feeling almost guilty for keeping Giovanni a secret once more. After all, they had been friends too.

1902

The kids were asleep for the night, as was Lorenzo. Our guests, The Alto Family, were now with us for a couple of weeks. I couldn't fall asleep for some reason, perhaps because Giovanni was still on my mind. I decided to walk out to the patio from the kitchen area and sit down on one of the chairs. It was a clear warm summer night.

"Do you believe that the stars are all of our ancestors that have passed on, looking down at us?" Giovanni walked out onto the patio holding a small glass of port, "May I?" He gestured towards one of the other chairs nearby.

"Of course, please." I sat up so as not look so relaxed in front of a man. "Oh, I don't know what the stars are. I would like to think that of course. Maybe knowing one day that we will be up there to watch over our family and yet still be with other loved ones when we die might make dying a little easier."

I realized that I was rambling on and looked over at Giovanni who was looking right at me. Thank goodness it was dark out, otherwise he would have seen my face blushing. For some reason, even though he was there for a couple of weeks now, I still got nervous around him. Giovanni's eyes made my stomach ache. It would almost make me cry knowing I could not have him. I never wanted something so much before, never wanted to hold someone like that. Be held by him.

"My grandmother from my mother's side told me when I was a little boy, right after my grandfather passed away, that grandpa was looking down at us. She would always point to a star and say 'you see, there he is'. She would use it against me of course for when I was being bad. She would say 'Giovanni! Nonno is looking at you and he knows the truth!'" Giovanni laughed.

We spent the next twenty minutes or so talking of our childhood. It was nice to laugh a little.

I eventually got up. "It's getting late and I should turn in now. Goodnight Giovanni."

"Bouna sera Luisa." Giovanni stood up and looked at me with the same longing that I had for him. We both knew it would not be good to be seen together so late at night. He had such a defeated look on his face. It's almost as if I could read his mind. It was as if he was telling me he wished things could have been different.

I looked back at him with understanding, smiled then turned and walked away.

****

"Luisa! We are here!"

Days later, they arrived in New York City. Giuseppe's friend, Francesco, was to meet them there. He held a sign up with their last name. Michael saw it right away and waved to him. A balding short

45

man with a thick mustache and a great big smile acknowledged Michael's wave and headed straight towards them.

"Hello, Luisa? Michael? Francesco Bartoloni." He put his hand out for them to shake. "Welcome to New Yorka!"

Francesco had his Italian accent still, but both Luisa and Michael were used to that. It seemed to be different and a bit harsher then what they were used to. Michael told Luisa on the train how New Yorkers had a certain way of talking. They laughed at Michael's impressions of the average New Yorker. Francesco had a mix of both New York and Italian, which they found to be amusing.

"I can't tell you how appreciative to you I am for helping us." Luisa shook his hand.

"Oh, anythinga for my friend Giuseppe."

They walked to the car and put all the luggage in the back trunk and got into the car.

As they drove to his house, Francesco told them all the exciting things that New York has to offer.

"You gatta be careful when you walk arounda here. You dun know someone might trya take you bag from you. It's not like where youa from you know. Here you gatta be very careful, understand?"

He also told her about the position he got for her at the local tailor. Luisa had known all about sewing and had even made some clothes for the children over the years. They were planning on heading into the city in a few days after settling down. He offered Michael a job to help at his fruit and vegetable store while Michael figured out how he would get a job at The New York Times. Francesco told him he might want to start at some smaller newspaper companies but Michael said he was willing to work in the mailroom if need be. He was going right to the main source. They both laughed at his confidence.

The house was a three story attached brick building. Francesco showed them the downstairs area where they would be staying. Luisa loved it. It was so different then where they stayed at the vineyard. It was more modern although much smaller. It was one long room with a bathroom but enough room for the both of them. There were two beds, each against a different wall to the back by the small windows. In the middle there was a couch, and a small table and chair set nearby. Then on the other end was a counter that acted as the kitchen, which included a small sink and some cabinets. A bathroom was against the wall at the other end.

"When you are settled a little pleasea come upstairs, my wife, she prepara nice meal. I'm sure both a ya are very tired after long trip.

If you rather take a nap first, that's ok too." Francesco looked at Luisa waiting for an answer.

"Oh we would love to have a bite to eat first. Thank you very much. We will wash up and be there in a few minutes if that is alright?"

"Yes, very good! Just come uppa stairs and the door is open."

They both opened their luggage and unpacked a few items. Taking turns in the bathroom while the other put more stuff away. When they were finished, they headed upstairs to the main floor. You could hear loud talking from inside the room where the door was open.

"Hello?" Luisa slowly stepped into the room. A plump woman with a large smile immediately greeted her with extended arms.

"Yes, come in! Come in! We wait for you." Francesco came over and introduced his wife and two younger children to them. He then went to the table and came over with two glasses of wine. After everyone had a glass, he raised it. "To a new friends! A Salute!"

They all touched glasses and continued with conversation and a wonderful meal. Luisa could tell that this was a nice family and one she was happy to stay with while in New York. She felt very safe. After the meal, they headed back downstairs to unpack and get some sleep. Michael was already determined to get started on getting a job at *The New York Times* and spent most of his night thinking out a plan and reading the local newspaper that Mr. Bartoloni gave him earlier.

The next few days, the Bartoloni family showed Luisa and Michael the local stores and how to get around via bus and subway. It was the springtime and they were looking forward to an interesting summer. Mrs. Bartoloni took Luisa shopping for some clothes. Giuseppe had given her enough money to get a few things and would be sending her money each month as needed until she seemed financially settled.

The following week Luisa started her new job at the tailor. The owner seemed nice enough although a bit loud when things didn't go his way. She sat in a back room along with four other people, three women and one man. Luisa proved to be a hard worker and they all got along very well. She became close to one of the women there, Sara. Sara always made Luisa laugh and really made the day go by quick. She wondered why she didn't think to come to New York sooner. There was so much more to do and more ways to spend her day than back on the vineyard. Many times, Sara would invite Luisa and Michael over with some other friends on the weekend. Michael was happy with this because Sara had a son around his age and they would sometimes go out themselves for the night. Michael even met a few of the local girls. The girls were different from where he lived back in California. These girls seemed to be more confident which he found interesting, and it didn't hurt that they were beautiful too.

Michael had sent his resume to The New York Times but had not heard back from them. To his surprise, he wasn't in as much of a rush as he thought he would be. He really enjoyed his days at the store with Mr. Bartoloni and seeing his new friends every night.

One day, Luisa's boss, Vito, came to her to let her know that one of their important clients was coming in with a suit that needed tailoring and said she would need to assist him as the others had projects that needed to be finished. After about an hour or so, she heard the bell ring to the entrance of the store and assumed it would be the man she was to help. Vito called for her to come up front.

"Perhaps he will be your prince charming, eh?" Sara laughed. Luisa threw a piece of fabric at her as she walked towards the front of the store.

When she pulled back the curtain Luisa actually stopped walking. The man standing there in front of her was a very handsome man indeed. She had never seen someone up close that well put together from top to bottom. His dark hair was slicked back and neat, his face was like a clay Greek sculpture with a perfectly square jaw line. He had blue eyes that were as clear as the ocean. Even the suit he wore was made of the best fabric and fit to perfection. He was impeccable. When he saw Luisa come out he gave her a warm smile. The smile made Luisa melt even more. She put her hand up. "Excuse me, one moment please." She then went back to the area Sara was sitting.

"What is it Luisa?" Sara looked worried.

"He is the most beautiful man I have ever seen!" Luisa looked surprised as if it wasn't possible to look so good.

"Oh Luisa, go out there and enjoy it before he leaves and has someone else fix his suit! Vito might call Frank to do it! Go!" She laughed as she nudged Luisa back out through the curtain.

"Hi, I'm Luisa. I believe you have a suit that needs to be altered?"

"Yes I do, hello Luisa. My name is Samuel. It's a pleasure to meet you." Samuel put his hand out to shake Luisa's.

Vito looked at the both of them and walked away rolling his eyes at the obvious flirtation.

Luisa smiled. "Sir, please use this room to put the suit on. When you are done you can go over to that mirror there and I will be right with you."

"Thank you," he said, and headed to the small dressing room.

When Samuel came out, he headed over to the mirror and stepped up onto a large round stool. As Luisa made the adjustments with her chalk and pins, Samuel asked her some questions. She noticed there was no ring on his finger, and blushed that she had even looked.

Some men do not wear wedding rings, so it could mean nothing, she thought to herself. She shook her head and focused on her work.

"So Luisa, I have never seen you here before. Are you new?"

Luisa kept looking at the suit as she pinned. "Yes, I just started a couple weeks ago. I moved here from California. My family owns a vineyard there."

"Really? So why would you leave it? Sounds lovely." Samuel laughed a little but Luisa just smiled.

"I needed a change I suppose."

Luisa proceeded to answer all of his questions about how she came to America from Sicily when she was younger. That was the story she told everyone at least. She would love to have asked him questions herself but dared not be so forward. When they were done, Samuel went to the room to change back into the outfit he walked in with. On his way, he stopped and turned towards her. "By any chance, would you like to go to dinner this evening?"

She heard Vito mumble something, but ignored him. "Yes that would be nice. Thank you."

"Wonderful, does six thirty work? Where shall I pick you up?" He looked at Vito almost for approval.

Vito answered for her. "She lives down the block." He then wrote down her address handing it to Samuel. Everyone felt it their job to take care of Luisa, and since Vito knew Samuel as a client he didn't think it would be a problem.

Later that evening, Luisa got ready and put on one of her new dresses that she bought while shopping with Mrs. Bartoloni. She heard the doorbell ring upstairs and Mr. Bartoloni called down for her to let her know that her guest had arrived.

"Would you like glass of wine?" he asked Samuel.

"That would be great but actually I have reservations that we shouldn't be late for. Maybe another time?" Samuel shook his hand.

"Ok, very good, Luisa you be careful. We wait up." Mr. Bartoloni told them.

"I will take very good care of her no need to worry." Samuel smiled at the couple.

They walked outside towards his car. She was a little nervous. Vito had told Luisa earlier that Samuel was one of his best clients. In other words, he had a lot of money. He worked as a stockbroker in the city. Luisa wondered why he wasn't married. Samuel wasn't old but usually men were married at his age. She guessed he was in his mid 30s and figured she would find more out as the night progressed.

"I hope you're ok with going into the city tonight. I know a great restaurant with entertainment. Wonderful singer, he's a client of mine."

"That sounds lovely." That seemed to be all Luisa could say. She didn't want to embarrass herself. Truth was she was extremely excited, although at first Luisa was nervous at the mention of heading into the city. When she went with the Bartoloni's into the city for the first time she was taken back at how run down it was. Mr. Bartoloni cautioned her never to go there alone. It was too dangerous for a young woman all by herself. There was no need for him to worry, she had no plans of ever doing that. She felt safe with Samuel though. He lived in the city so he would know the right places to go.

Luisa didn't like to think this way but a part of her wished Lorenzo was here to share it with her. It has been so long but she still thinks of him and remembers how hard he worked and how well he took care of her. It would have been nice for him to enjoy life a little more himself. She felt guilty being with another man and having a good time. However, if her children understood then she felt she was doing no wrong. Again, so much time had passed. It was silly of her to think that way and she got the thought out of her head quickly.

When they arrived at the restaurant, a young man opened the door for her and helped her out. Samuel came around to meet her and shook the boy's hand. He put his arm out for her to hold as they proceeded to enter the restaurant.

"Mr. Roberts, how are you this evening?" Another man greeted him at the door.

"Good and yourself?" Samuel asked with familiarity.

At that moment, yet another man escorted them through the restaurant. The music was getting louder as they entered the room towards the back. There was a low stage to the side and on it, there was a man singing and playing the piano. When they walked past him, he nodded his head towards Samuel as if to say hi. Samuel responded with the same gesture.

The waiter showed them to their table, not too far from the stage. It was a perfect location with enough privacy if they chose not to watch the entertainment. The restaurant was dark and lit with just enough soft light surrounding them. Luisa had never been to a place so exquisite before. She wondered if her dress was fancy enough for the evening. It's a good thing Mrs. Bartoloni lent her a necklace that dressed it up a bit more.

The waiter pulled the chair out for her and after they sat down, he handed them both a menu.

"You will love the food here. Anything you order is terrific." Samuel was smiling at her. She still couldn't believe how handsome he was.

Luisa looked at the menu and she hoped he didn't see her expression. There were no prices on the menu, which worried her. She wasn't sure exactly what she should get and usually went by the price when someone else was buying her dinner. She would pick the least expensive item on the menu.

Luisa decided she would strike up a conversation this time. "So Samuel, what line of work do you do?" She knew the answer to this thanks to her boss Vito but figured best to hear it first hand from Samuel.

"I'm a Partner at a small investment banking firm. A couple of my buddies from college decided we should open our own firm. Turns out we knew what we were doing." Samuel found that funny. "Been doing it for the past ten years now."

"Did you grow up in Manhattan?" Luisa couldn't imagine being a child growing up in the city. It didn't seem peaceful at all. She started to feel bad for him just picturing a young Samuel in such a hectic environment compared to life on the vineyard.

"I grew up in Queens actually, not far from where you are living now. My parents still live there."

The waiter came by to take their wine order. Samuel picked one of the best bottles on the list. They started talking about wines which Luisa knew a lot about. This impressed Samuel since most women he knew didn't know much about wine at all.

The evening turned out to be a great night. Luisa really enjoyed being with Samuel and took comfort in the fact that he seemed to be a kind man with well manners and in no way made her feel uncomfortable.

The night was close to ending. Samuel drove up to Luisa's house and helped her out of the car. He held her hand as they walked to the door.

"So do I get to see you again soon?" he asked her.

"I will have to check my calendar first." Luisa looked up to the sky. "Yes, ok I am available every night for the next month." They both laughed.

"I was hoping for longer than that but for now, I'll take a month." He kissed her on the cheek and waited until she was safely inside before walking back to his car.

When Luisa closed the door, Mr. Bartoloni's door opened. "Luisa? Is everything ok?"

She could hear his wife yelling from the background. "Let her be!" She came from behind her husband and whispered, "But tell us all about it tomorrow, eh?"

Mrs. Bartoloni winked at her before gently pushing her husband away from the door. "Goodnight, Luisa."

Luisa just laughed and headed down to her apartment where Michael was already sleeping. That night she slept with a smile on her face. It has been a while since Luisa felt that life had something to offer her again, and she planned to enjoy it.

The next day she was woken by the phone ringing and quickly got up to answer it knowing Michael would be in a dead sleep. Sure enough, he didn't even flinch.

"Hello?"

"So…tell me all about your night!" Sara laughed.

"If I could wake up first I will! What time is it anyway?"

"Time for you to tell me all of last night's details!" Sara wasn't going to hang up until she got what she wanted.

"I'll tell you what. Let me wake up and open my eyes. We can meet for lunch and I will be more than happy to tell you everything."

"Pizzeria at noon." Sara hung-up without a goodbye. There was only one pizza place they all went to so she knew which one she meant. Carlo's had the best pizza in town.

Luisa walked to the kitchen area, filled the espresso maker with coffee and put it on the stove. She knew once Michael smelled the coffee he would get up as well. She then headed to the bathroom to get ready for her lunch date with Sara.

When she arrived she saw that Sara had already been sitting at a booth and waved to her.

"How long have you been here?" Luisa asked.

"Long enough, now start talking." Sara wanted all details.

"What about food! Am I allowed to eat at least?" Luisa headed to the counter to place an order. Sara followed and they both ordered a slice and small soda.

"I bet you ate better than this last night!" Sara laughed but then smiled at Carlo after seeing the dirty look he gave her.

Luisa ignored her and waited until they were back at their table to talk. She didn't think it was anyone else's business what she did last night. As fun as Sara was, she was a little too forward and loud for Luisa sometimes. She was, however, grateful for Sara in her life. At the moment she was her closest friend.

"Finally. Now where did he take you?" Sara asked, before taking a big bite of her pizza.

"We went to a nice fancy restaurant in the city. Don't ask me where because I couldn't tell you, I have no idea. I just know it was really nice and probably really expensive."

Sara smiled big raising her eyebrows, liking the story so far.

"I asked him about himself, you know, what he does, where he grew up, what his favorite food is…"

"You asked him what his favorite food was?" Sara looked at Luisa like she had two heads.

"Yes, what's wrong with that?"

"Luisa, sounds to me like you were interviewing the man. Haven't you been on dates before?" Sara looked right at Luisa waiting for an answer knowing that she actually might not have been.

"Anyway," Luisa shook her head in annoyance. "After dinner he took me home and asked if he could see me again and I said yes. I don't know why, but I figured why not."

Sara continued to look at Luisa, which made her feel uncomfortable.

"That's it?"

"Yes, what else would there be?" Luisa took a sip of her soda hoping this conversation would end.

Sara seemed to give in and stopped pushing her. "So do you like him?"

"He's really nice." Luisa took a bite of her pizza looking down at her plate while she chewed, knowing Sara was looking at her still.

"Ok, I'm just going to ask. Was there a man in your past that you can't get over? It's just I can tell. You never mentioned anything before, but every time I see a man look at you and smile you look the other way. I thought for sure I was wrong when you decided to go out with Samuel but I can hear it in your voice that you aren't excited about this at all. I mean you act like you just went to dinner with Vito or something. You went to dinner with a really handsome man who seems to really like you, Luisa. So who was he? The guy that caused you not to let anyone else in your life."

Luisa was taken back by Sara's question. "Just because I am not acting like a teenager in high school doesn't mean anything Sara!"

"Were you ever in a long relationship with anyone before?" Sara wanted an answer as always. She wasn't going to quit asking.

Luisa thought for a moment. Sure she was married to Lorenzo and had a wonderful life. One that she would never change. Yet, for some reason the person who she thought of right away was Giovanni. Why was it that the short time she spent with him seemed to have more of an impact on her than all the years with Lorenzo?

As soon as Luisa thought of Giovanni, Sara sensed it. She knew that there was someone always on Luisa's mind. Only she could never imagine how long ago that was.

"Don't be silly, Sara." Luisa dismissed her and took another bite of her pizza.

Sara could see that Luisa was not going to open up. "Luisa, remember one thing, you came to New York for a new start. At least that's what you told me. At least enjoy it and start already."

Sara was right. How long can she hold on to her memories of Giovanni? It was so long ago, and it would never result in anything other than what it was. Giovanni was gone, Lorenzo was gone—Luisa was alone, holding tight to two ghosts. Perhaps Sara was right after all. If she is going to be on this earth for however long she might as well have someone to enjoy it with. So she decided, she would finally put the past to rest.

Chapter 9

Luisa had been seeing Samuel for over a month now. They would go to nightclubs in the city or dinner locally. Luisa cooked for him on a few occasions as well and he was very impressed. But what impressed him most was her tailoring. Samuel liked to dress to impress, wore the best suits, and used only the finest materials. Luisa convinced him to let her make him his own custom suit. He had his assistant order fine material and Luisa fitted him and made the suit. The evening he tried it on Samuel couldn't believe how wonderful it had turned out.

Later that evening after Samuel left, Michael and Luisa were talking about the suit.

"You really made a great impression on Sammy with that suit Luisa. I don't think he believed you make a suit like that." Michael was talking as he ate some leftover desert that Luisa brought back for him.

"Well what do you expect, after 60 years of experience and no arthritis I had better make a great suit!" They both laughed. "And you better not let him hear you calling him Sammy!"

****

One Saturday afternoon, Samuel took Luisa to lunch at an outdoor cafe in the city. There was one smaller table in the corner and the waiter escorted them to it. Luisa noticed to her left two women sitting together had stopped talking and looked right at Samuel with wide eyes. She was getting used to that. He was a handsome man and she loved the attention.

"Shall I order us a bottle of red?" Samuel looked at her for approval.

"Sounds good to me, Cabernet perhaps?"

The waiter put a basket of bread on the table and Luisa quickly grabbed a piece. All she had was a cup of coffee in the morning and a cookie.

The waiter brought over the bottle of wine that Samuel picked out from the list, opened it and poured a sample for him to taste before proceeding. After the waiter left they clicked their glasses together before drinking.

"Luisa, I have been doing some thinking. With your talent, you could really be successful with your own tailoring shop. You know, custom made suits. I have a large clientele that I know would appreciate the fine work. I could help you out financially. There are plenty of shops here downtown that are for lease maybe we could become partners? What do you say?"

Luisa was taken back. "Oh, well, I don't know. I never thought about that. My own business? What if I fail?" Luisa looked worried. In her day, the men worked and ran businesses of their own. She had to accept that times have been changing and she should be changing with them.

"Come on, with me on your side the word failure does not exist!" Samuel was a smart man and she knew that he was right. With her talent, he could help her run the business. Maybe one day make enough money to buy a house with Michael.

"Wow. Ok, why not? Let's go for it!" She was excited about the idea now.

"Excellent!" Samuel sounded extremely pleased at her decision.

That night, Luisa explained to Michael what Samuel told her and he, being young and ambitious, saw it as a great opportunity for her.

The following week Samuel took Luisa around to show her some empty shops for rent. She told him all that she needed as far as supplies and he said he would take care of it. Her boss was sad to see her go but knew himself that Luisa was too talented to be working in the back of his store.

When they finally agreed on a place to rent, they spent all month fixing it up with paint and filling it with the supplies needed. Luisa felt so important. Years ago, she would never have her own business like this. Women sat back and the men did the work. They had the businesses, not the wives.

She saw so many changes over the years of how women really became stronger in the world. That was one good thing about her being around so long. She couldn't believe that Lorenzo wasn't able to see all of this.

Lorenzo.

It seemed like another lifetime that she was with him. Sometimes she even had to convince herself it wasn't a dream and her life on the vineyard was, in fact, real. She thought about Giovanni also. Even Samuel didn't make her feel the way Giovanni did. It was too bad the way things turned out. However, she accepted her life for what it was and decided to take advantage of all opportunities that came her way.

****

Luisa and Samuel spent a lot more time together as a couple. She would spend many nights at his loft in SoHo and it seemed to be fine with the Bartoloni's and Michael, considering she was old enough to make her own decisions. They also liked Samuel very much and trusted him with Luisa.

The first night they spent together was about a month after they had been dating. Sara told her that she needed to get going or she was going to lose Samuel. Sara would call her a prude and tell her that she was a woman in New York City now and she had to show it or sit back. Luisa could not believe how quickly women went to sleep with men these days. She also realized that she was old enough at this point and did not want to lose Samuel's interest. One night instead of doing the usual after a night out, which would be him driving her home, she told Samuel in the car that she would like to stay over his place. Samuel respected Luisa and was pleased that it was her idea and not his. The night was probably the most romantic she had ever had with a man. Samuel placed candles all around the room and soft music played in the background. He was very gentle and slow with Luisa knowing that she was special and not like most women. He truly respected her for that. After that night, Luisa was much more comfortable with Samuel and he convinced her to stay over more often.

Luisa loved spending time there. Some nights they would host cocktail parties with friends. It was the most fun she ever had. She felt like she was living the life of a movie star with the fancy dresses and a very handsome man on her arm. Things were very good for her now.

Every week her and Michael called Giuseppe and the rest of the family to let them know how things were going.

Michael ended up getting a job at *The New York Times*. It was a small position, but a foot in the door, and he loved it. Luisa's business was growing daily. Giuseppe could not believe how successful things were going for them both and was relieved that he had decided to send them away.

Chapter 10

Luisa enjoyed having the business and was making plenty of new friends, including a woman named Helen. She was dating Samuel's friend, Max. They had been dating for a little over five years. She was down to earth and made Luisa laugh. Some nights, when Max and Samuel were working late, or attending business dinners, the two of them would get together.

One night, Luisa decided to invite Helen to Samuel's loft for dinner. As Luisa was cooking in the open kitchen, Helen lit two cigarettes and handed Luisa one of them.

"I think the men want to go out this Friday night to one of the night clubs with a group of people." Helen took a long drag of her cigarette. "What do you think?"

"I think it sounds like fun and something different for a change," Luisa answered. They normally just went out alone and she wondered why they never met up with all the other friends she would hear Samuel talk about constantly.

"You know, I should warn you Luisa, some of these people we hang out with can get a little crazy. I have a feeling you might not be used to that."

Luisa stopped stirring her risotto. "What do you mean by *crazy*?"

"Oh I don't know, they like to party let's just keep it at that. You will see Friday night."

****

The week seemed to go fast and Luisa was getting ready for her night out. She went shopping with Sara after looking in her closet. When she told Sara they were going to a nightclub for some dancing Sara convinced her she would need something special to wear.

Luisa never saw herself dressed so sexy before. Helen came by that night to help with her hair and makeup. Luisa felt a little foolish but decided she needed to keep up with the times. She knew she was looking a little too proper compared to the other women her age.

When she came out to the living area, Samuel whistled. "Holy crap you look awesome!" He grabbed her close to him and gave her a kiss.

"Watch the make up! Helen worked hard on it!"

Max clapped his hands hard and loud, a cigarette hanging from the side of his mouth. "Let's go!"

They pulled up to a club with a long line and blue lights on the outside. It was definitely an area of town she had never seen before.

Samuel whispered in her ear, "Don't worry baby, we are going to have a good time tonight, ok?" He kissed her on the cheek.

For some reason Luisa was feeling nervous. She was not used to this kind of life style. Everything seemed loud and fast paced. They went to the front of the line and were let in immediately. Obviously Max knew the owner. Someone escorted them through the nightclub. The music was loud and both Max and Samuel were saying hello to people as they walked through towards the back. They seemed to know everyone, or at least everyone knew them.

There they were seated at a booth, filled with drinking people. Once they saw Samuel, the men got up and all shook hands. Over the loud music, he introduced Luisa to everyone. Drinks were poured and Samuel handed her a clear drink on ice.

He saw her expression. "Luisa, there are other things to drink besides wine!"

She accepted it. The drink was a bit too strong for her taste but she took small sips, and kept smiling.

They all did some dancing throughout the night that Luisa discovered she loved. She never felt so wild and free. Times sure were different than they used to be. She laughed at the thought of Lorenzo trying to dance here. She couldn't even picture it in her head. They returned to the table and one of Samuels friends handed him something. She had no idea what it was. Samuel looked over at Luisa and smiled and turned back again bending over to do something. She just wasn't sure what. Then he came closer to Luisa with what looked like a mirror in his hand and white powder lined up on the top.

"What is that?" Luisa asked, not looking interested.

"This will make you feel really good and have a great time. I'll show you what to do." She watched him take a small tube and place it at the end of his nose and in an instant, he sniffed up a line of the white powder.

"Samuel! What is that? What on earth are you doing?"

"It's cocaine, Luisa. Everyone is doing it."

59

She heard of it before but never actually saw it. Luisa was too scared to do anything like that and motioned with her hand saying, "No thanks."

Max looked at Samuel who returned the glance in disappointment. Both men returned to the table and did another line. Their pupils huge, smiles goofy and hands more forward than they normally were in public.

Luisa didn't like the way Samuel was acting the rest of the night. It was so strange to her. She decided to stop drinking because everyone else around her seemed to be in his or her own little world and it wasn't a place she wanted to join.

When they arrived home that evening Samuel was clearly in a bad mood.

"Are you feeling ok?" she asked him.

"I'm fine. Listen, these are my friends and I feel like you don't really want to have fun with them. They are good people Luisa," he said while getting undressed.

"What are you talking about? I never said anything bad about them Samuel! They seem fine." She was surprised by his comment.

"That's just it. They are *fine*. You looked at them in judgment all night Luisa." He seemed disgusted.

She realized where this was going. "Listen, just because I chose not to do things that anyone else does I am not judging them. I don't care what they do. I had a good time."

They went to bed that night with anger in the air. She started to wonder if perhaps Samuel wasn't the man she thought he was.

The next day everything was fine and back to normal as if Samuel forgot it all. She was glad about that. He seemed to be his normal self again.

Two weeks later, he told her they were invited to a friend's house for a party that Saturday. She was excited to go and hoped it wouldn't be like their last night out with friends. Apparently, she met this couple at the nightclub but couldn't remember them.

The apartment was not far from where they lived. At first things seemed to be fine until the night progressed. Most of the lights were low and again things started to be passed around. Everyone was sitting around on the couches or floor; it was all getting too casual and Luisa was starting to feel uncomfortable again. Samuel did not push her to do anything. In fact, he didn't even offer anything to her only the occasional glass of white wine they had made sure to bring at Luisa's request.

Luisa started to feel funny after her second drink. It was as if the room was melting on one side and she was starting to float along. All she could hear was laughter in the background and feel Samuel kissing her on her cheek.

She thought she was seeing things at first. It seemed as though one of the girls was on the floor naked. She assured herself she must have been wrong but was finding it so hard to focus. The next thing she knew there was a hand unbuttoning her blouse and it all was so quick but that hand was fondling her breast. She slowly looked over, confused and saw it was Samuel. Why would he do this in front of everyone? She tried to stop him with her hands but it was impossible and all her arms were capable of doing was falling to the sides. He then started to kiss her neck and what was strange is she swore someone was touching her legs but she knew his hands were on her breasts so how could that be?

The rest of the night was a blur. She couldn't remember anything. All she could remember was Samuel placing her in their bed and waking up the next morning.

He was already out of bed and drinking coffee at the table in the dining area.

She got up, covered herself up with a robe, and walked over to him.

"Samuel, what happened last night? I can't remember. I didn't drink much. I remember feeling really funny." She was too embarrassed to say the few things she did remember.

He was reading the paper and didn't even look up to her as he said, "You just drank a little too much, and it's ok."

Luisa didn't feel comfortable. In the future when Samuel mentioned a party with their friends, she said she wasn't feeling well. He must have understood because he stopped asking and they would spend more time alone or just with Max and Helen, which was fine by her.

It was one thing to understand that times were not the same but there were certain things she also knew she did not have to go along with in these times. Luisa realized she was to make decisions on her own now. Lorenzo and Giuseppe were no longer here to protect her. The men of today were so different then the men of her time. The respect for women changed, as did women's thinking. It was as if they too lost some sort of respect for themselves. Samuel wanted Luisa to move in with him but she knew that was something she would not change her mind about ever. Unless they were married, she was going to continue to live with Michael in the apartment.

Samuel started to understand that Luisa was not like the other women and even he stopped going out with certain friends. His feelings for her were stronger than he thought and trying to change her was foolish on his part. Luisa might not have known it but Samuel actually did respect her, more than she thought.

****

Over a year went by. Luisa's tailoring business flourished. Samuel was able to send all of his clients to her and as expected they were all very impressed with her work. One night he decided to take her out to dinner to celebrate their success. He booked a reservation at their favorite restaurant and picked her up as usual. It was a hot night and the summer was ending. She wore a simple yellow dress, one of Samuels's favorites. Even though it was warm, Samuel still wore a jacket. He always made sure to dress sharp telling her people judge you by the way you dress.

They ordered a bottle of sparkling wine to start with.

"Luisa, you really are the most extraordinary woman I have ever met. As I've told you over the years, I just never had time to get close to anyone. Truth is I never found anyone that I really wanted to get close *to*. I worked more hours than ever just to keep busy. Since I met you I enjoy life more and I look forward to the time we spend together." He took her hand into his. "Luisa, I'd like to ask you to marry me. I love you so much and I want to see your face every night when I get home and spend every minute with you that I possibly can."

At this, Luisa's eyes filled with tears of joy. Never did she think she could ever find love again. She did with Samuel. Luisa wanted nothing more than to be with him for the rest of her life. However, at that thought she realized something else as well. The rest of her life? What did that really mean? In her case, that could mean a very long time. Possibly forever. How could she ever begin to explain this to him? It's not something you can just tell someone like its normal. It's not normal and it's not something she can give full answers to. She was just as confused about all of this as anyone else.

Samuel saw her expression turn from joy to sorrow. This tore at his heart. He honestly thought this through and couldn't think of any reason why Luisa would not want to marry him. She explained to him already how she really did not have any family close by. They were all in California with the exception of Michael, her younger brother. He knew that the majority of women he knew of would have done anything to be in her position. So the question now was what was in her head? What could she possibly be thinking?

"Oh Samuel, I've been in love with you from the moment we met. I feel like the luckiest woman right now. All I ask is that you let me think about this. I don't want to hurt you but I really have a complicated life right now. I can't explain it." Luisa had tears streaming down her face.

"Complicated? Luisa, we have known each other now for almost two years. I thought we were perfectly honest with each other, with everything! You seemed to be happy with me. If there is a reason you don't want to marry me please, all I ask is for you to be honest. I can handle it. Just don't tell me stories." Samuel seemed upset and was getting more angry than hurt. Insulted was probably more like it. Usually, men like Samuel got what they wanted. He couldn't understand what was happening and thought it was a no brainer that they should get married. But he was wrong.

The rest of the evening was extremely awkward. Neither spoke much and rushed through their meal without finishing their plates. The waiter, who has known them over the years, knew better than to strike up any conversation. The tension in the air was thick. He handed Samuel the check and wished them a pleasant evening without extra small talk.

In the car ride home, Luisa tried to say something to break the silence. She was so worried of hurting Samuels's feelings and started to wonder if she did the right thing. Maybe she should have just accepted the proposal and could have dealt with everything day by day. She did it for years with Lorenzo. They managed to fool everyone for quite a while. The difference was Lorenzo knew her secret. Moreover, would that be even worse to do to Samuel? To have to leave after ten years of falling even deeper in love with each other? What if he wanted to have children? She really had feelings for him and she knew a man like himself would think she was out of her mind if she even tried to explain her situation. It would ruin their relationship without a doubt.

"Samuel, I don't want you to be upset with me." She couldn't even look at him.

"Don't go there, Luisa. Really, it's ok."

Clearly it wasn't. Samuel felt defeated for the first time and it showed that he did not know how to handle it. Again, he usually succeeded in everything. This one was a big surprise to him. He was a confident man, always had been, which explained his success. In his mind, it was just something he would deal with. He figured everything out. Although this time, for a brief moment, he wasn't sure how.

Chapter 11

That evening Luisa waited up for Michael to get home. He had been seeing a girl he met at work, which Luisa loved and approved of.

The second Luisa heard the door she stood up waiting for him to come down the stairs.

"Jeeze! What are you doing standing there? You scared me half to death. Why are you up so late anyway?" Michael continued down the stairs taking off his jacket and looking at Luisa with suspicion.

"Michael. I think I have to leave. It's time." She knew it was not something Michael wanted to hear but said it with authority. She knew he was living his dreams right now and part of her felt bad for breaking this news to him.

"Excuse me? It's time? Time for what? I'm not going anywhere, Luisa!" He stopped and looked at her more serious now. "Did something happen? Like, are you sick or something?" He now looked worried and felt bad for his initial reaction. It was also his job to look after Luisa. He promised his grandfather. He realized at that moment that he wasn't really doing his job and perhaps thinking only of himself.

Life seemed to be going so good for them both that there was never anything to be worried about. Or so he thought.

"No. I'm fine. I mean my health is fine. It's just, Samuel. He asked me to marry him. How am I supposed to do that? How am I supposed to grow old with him which is what he expects? What will happen? Oh, why must this happen to me? I just don't understand this!" Luisa's hands were flying in the air out of anger now.

"Listen, Luisa, if this didn't happen to you, you wouldn't even be here right now. You never would have met Sammy so let's just relax and think about this." He sat down at the table thinking. "Ok, so you marry him and we will tell him in a few years. I can have Nonno come and talk to him just like he told all of us."

"Oh Michael, it's not that simple! Samuel is a very intelligent man! He will not listen to such a thing, as true as it might be. He will want nothing to do with me at that point. He will think we are just crazy." She sat at the table next to him and looked him in the eyes not sure what he would think of what she was about to say next.

"I have been thinking of something lately. I mean, I know it seems I have done so much already. A business and everything but so

64

far I'm still...young." Michael nodded, encouraging her to go on. "I was thinking of going to college to get a degree. Be more than someone who makes suits! This would be a perfect opportunity for me to go away. I've saved enough money to go." She looked at him sadly. "Although I'm sorry, I was hoping to buy us a home of our own with that money."

Michael laughed. "It's ok. I think that sounds like a nice idea and don't worry about me. I'm older now you know. I don't need anyone taking care of me. I'm thinking of asking Katherine to marry me one day soon. I really think I'll be getting a better position at the paper and I've been saving money myself. Even if we live here for a bit, I'm sure Mr. Bartoloni will be ok with that. Then, I'll save for a house, for Katherine and I. That is, if she marries me." He laughed sadly, thinking of Luisa's rejection of Samuel.

They hugged each other and spent the next hour or so talking about their plans for the coming year. Michael agreed to take Luisa the following week to register for the university in Upstate, New York. She wanted to stay close enough to Michael so that he wasn't alone on the east coast. Luisa spent the next day on the phone explaining to her son, Giuseppe that this was indeed a good idea for her. She had all the time in the world, so she might as well put that time to good use. It was hard for him to understand. After all, the world was changing. More and more women were attending college and becoming more independent. He told her how his father would never hear of such a thing but that he himself understood what she was going through and wished her well. Giuseppe was getting older now and he seemed to be much more laid back.

Samuel bought Luisa's share of the business and hired a couple of tailors to run the shop. Luisa had to meet with him to finalize some paperwork at his office in the city. Samuel was not pleasant to her at all. In fact, she decided not to tell him her plans and instead mentioned that she would be moving back to California to stay with her family and help on the vineyard.

As Luisa got up to leave, she tried her best not to look him in the eye for fear of crying. Samuel was a great man. It was too bad things could not work out between them. It wouldn't be fair to either of them to keep this relationship going any longer. What they had was wonderful and would always be a part of her. Although, in her heart, as much as she was falling for Samuel, he would never be her husband, Lorenzo, and never be her true love, Giovanni.

They walked towards the door together. Samuel put his hand on the doorknob to let her out but his hand stayed there longer than expected as he closed his eyes.

"Don't go Luisa." He looked her in the eyes then. "I can't bear to go another day without you in my life. What we had was so good and I know you felt the same. If I scared you away with my proposal then I take it back. We don't have to get married. We can keep things going the way they were. What do you say?"

Samuel looked defeated. He would never let anyone other than her see him that way. It tore her heart when she saw his face. For a second Luisa even wanted to forget going to the university and just stay with Samuel. She had a successful business and a wonderful man in her life. If only it were that simple. She knew they would only be more attached to each other over the years and things would get too complicated. Then what? He would want to have children eventually. She wasn't even sure if she *could* have children. Better to end this now and give Samuel a chance at a life with someone normal. Just the thought of that word upset her. She wasn't normal and that was just it. Why and for how much longer she didn't know. She had to make difficult decisions and the more she lived on this earth the more she was getting better at it.

Luisa wasn't sure of the right words to say to him at first but they just came out. "Samuel, I don't know what to say except you have really given me so much over these last couple of years. I can never forget you and for all good reasons. Right now, my life is not what you would expect and I can't really explain that to you. You need to find someone who wants the same things in life that you want."

"I told you I was willing to forget about the marriage proposal. I just want you in my life." He grabbed the back of her neck and pulled her towards him embracing her, like it was the last time he held her. Luisa stayed there, hugging him back until she eventually let go, opened the door and left without looking back. When she got to the elevator, she hit the down button about ten times until it finally came. After getting in and waiting for the doors to close, she finally let her emotions get the best of her and cried until she left the building.

****

The next few days she and Michael got everything settled as far as registering and finding a place on campus to live. Michael had attended college and was familiar with the entire process. Luisa packed up all of her belongings and helped Michael load it into Mr. Bartoloni's car. He lent it to them for the ride up there. The Bartoloni's were not thrilled with the idea of Luisa being at the University all alone. They always heard of the crimes against vulnerable women and tried to tell her it wasn't a good idea. They thought she was too old for school and should be settling down and having a family. They also thought she made a big mistake not marrying Samuel and could not understand her decision. She couldn't explain to them her true reason but assured them she would be fine and would check in periodically.

"Maybe I can call the office and get a few more days off. Just to make sure you're ok," Michael said, once they were done settling Luisa in. He looked very worried leaving her.

Luisa laughed at him and pushed him towards the car. "Come on now, Mr. Bartoloni will have the dogs out looking for you if you keep his car another day! Do not worry about me. I've lasted now for close to 100 years. I will be fine!"

Michael gave her a hug and a kiss and got into the car. Luisa stepped back and waved with a smile as he drove away. She said aloud, for only her to hear, "Well, here I go with my next adventure!" And walked towards her apartment.

Chapter 12

Campus life was great so far. She started to wonder why she didn't think of this sooner. She kept to herself for the most part and really concentrated on her studies. There was a local bus that took you to the closest town and there she found a dry cleaner that gave her a job doing alterations part time. She didn't mention to them the extent of her experience, in case they wouldn't hire her for the part time position.

She enjoyed all of her classes as well. They kept her busy and for the most part, she wanted to learn more and more. She was excelling in every subject as well. One night, she decided to bring her textbook along with her to study while eating a quick dinner in the main dining hall. The food there was a big adjustment for Luisa. Basically, it stunk. More than one occasion she wanted to get behind the counter and cook the kids a great meal but she knew that would not be possible. Instead, she frowned at her options and grabbed a bowl of pasta with sauce; in other words: noodles with ketchup.

"Human Anatomy and a bowl of pasta? I can see why you wouldn't want to eat any meat while studying." Luisa looked up to see a young boy with a tray in his hand and a very serious expression on his face. What he was lacking in looks, he obviously was not making up in personality.

"Sorry for interrupting." He realized she was looking at him strangely and he quietly sat at the table behind her.

Luisa felt bad since it was obvious this boy was not trying to pick her up or anything. She turned and faced him. "Oh no, please. It's no bother at all. It was I either read this or stare at the wall as I ate. Would you care to join me? I could use some company. It would sure beat reading this!" She pointed to her book. "There are plenty of chairs to choose from."

He looked at her suspiciously. "Are you sure?" He seemed to feel bad now.

"Yes, absolutely! It would be nice to have company. I don't want to overload myself with my studies. I need *some* sort of break! My name is Luisa by the way, pleased to meet you."

"Mitchell Roth." He got up from his table with his tray, chose a seat furthest away from Luisa at her table, and sat down.

"So are you a teacher here?" He didn't even look at her, just started to eat.

"No, actually I'm a student. I guess you can say I took some time off before heading to college," she laughed. Luisa did not feel threatened at all by Mitchell. She could tell he was in no way trying to pick her up. She was not interested in a social life at this time. Luisa still had Samuel on her mind and coming to college was a way for her to escape. She really just wanted to keep to herself, but meeting Mitchell felt different. Even if only for a short time, it was nice to have someone to talk to for a change. The girls in her classes all seemed to have their own friends. They were friendly enough but Luisa never bothered with them socially, or after classes.

"So what are you studying here, Mitchell?"

"Physics," Mitchell answered as he continued to eat. It wasn't out of shyness that he didn't look at Luisa. It seemed more that he didn't care.

"Oh, how interesting!" She was genuinely interested, but all he did was shrug.

"What about you?" He seemed bored with the entire conversation as he ate.

"Well, nothing exciting really. I thought I would get a degree in teaching perhaps, maybe mathematics. So, tell me, what got you interested in physics?" She was curious if this kid could actually help her figure out what was going on with her life.

"I guess I'm just really smart and it makes sense. I mean, I like it and everything. I want to learn more. It comes easy to me. Enough reasons?"

"Yes. Your parents must be proud of you; such an accomplishment!" She continued eating when she realized the conversation was not going to go very far. After about 15 minutes of awkwardness, she realized the time and decided to get back to her room.

"Well, it was a pleasure meeting you Mitchell. I hope we can have some more conversations in the future." At that, Luisa stood up and collected her stuff.

He looked up at her and actually seemed sad she was leaving.

"Well, I usually get dinner here every Tuesday and Thursday night, so maybe I will see you then." He handed the book to her that was on the table.

"Sounds great, I will see you soon then." Luisa left and headed back towards her dorm.

Luisa and Mitchell became friends over time. She realized he didn't have many friends, not because he didn't want them. It was more that he didn't have the patience for people who were not as smart or mature as he was. With Luisa, she was a smart woman who seemed to know a lot, which surprised him. She wasn't trying to compete with him, which most of his peers did. Luisa seemed pleasant and genuinely intrigued when he would discuss his own theories on science. He knew nothing romantic would come about their friendship, mostly due to their age difference. He could be himself around her and didn't get nervous like he would around other girls.

Luisa always picked Mitchell's brain. She was always wondering what he would think had she told him her entire story. Would he believe her? He was studying to be a scientist after all and all scientists need evidence, facts. What did she have to prove her story other than some photos that could just show nothing more than having a strong resemblance to her great grandmother? Although there was the proof that her body seemed to heal exceptionally fast. She could cut herself and he could see it with his own eyes. She would hate to lose him as a friend though. He might think she was out of her mind. Maybe she could incorporate it in her conversations with him slowly. He was always talking about the latest research. She decided to throw it out there one evening.

"So what do you think about all those science fiction stories and movies that are out now? Do you think it's possible for some of these things to really happen?" They were in the cafeteria having dinner. Tonight she decided to go for the hamburger, no cheese. Just ketchup, which she sadly admitted to getting addicted to. Of course, what would the hamburger be without fries on the side? None of this food was good for her figure. She noticed she had gained a few pounds.

He laughed as he ate shaking his head, "I will say some of these books and movies really have some creativity attached there. I mean why couldn't any of these things really happen if you think about it. We can't prove that they can, but we also can't prove that they can't. Fifty years ago, we wouldn't even dream about some of the things we know today. Who is to say that in another 50 years, 100 years even, we won't be traveling to another time? Another galaxy or universe even. We can't say for sure."

"How would you explain let's say... someone never growing old. I mean really, staying the same age for 50 years! In addition, their body just heals automatically if ever hurt? I think I saw it on a silly movie the other night."

"I would say you need to change the channel, but seriously, never grow old? A scientific explanation for that? I guess they can discover something that doesn't wear down our bodies over time. Anything overused will eventually fall apart. In the early 1800's the average person lived into his mid 30's. Now it's more like the mid 70's. That's more than double. Therefore, if the movie is supposed to be based on the future, considering it was a science fiction movie, I would assume that is the case. I guess if you look at the life expectancy over time that could actually happen. But my guess is eventually the body would give out."

"Mitchell. I would like to tell you something. I'm not crazy or out of my mind. I am being very honest with you. However, I ask that you please respect my privacy. I will share this with you and expect you to keep it to yourself. Can you promise me that?"

Mitchell stopped eating and wiped his face and hands with his napkin then looked at her very suspiciously. "Why do I feel like you did something I don't want to know about?"

"No, no nothing bad, nothing like that at all! Just promise me."

"You have my word." He still looked worried.

As she spoke, she looked at the table the entire time. "Ok, well, here goes, I was born in 1870. I lived in Sicily on a vineyard where I met my husband, Lorenzo. We married and had three children..." she stopped talking to look at his reaction.

Mitchell stopped being serious and sat back in his chair throwing his napkin on his plate and smiling. "You got me! That's a good one. So what are you doing, writing a story for your literature class? Are you actually thinking of writing a script? Interesting stuff, I'll give you that."

Luisa paused, knowing this was of no use. "Yes," she laughed. "I was just being silly."

He got up. "On that note, I need to run to class." He walked away stopped and turned towards her. "It's a good thing there is only a couple of more weeks left to school. I think maybe you need a break from the books. You should take a trip home for a little. Go visit your brother maybe. You know, summer break is coming up next week. Sounds like you should take advantage."

That summer, Luisa convinced Michael to take a mini vacation. She suggested he bring Katherine along as well. Luisa didn't want to spend the break back in Queens. She was not in the mood to face the Bartoloni's and their many questions. They rented a small house on the water out on Long Island. It was very small but it was enough to accommodate the three of them. Luisa took a bus back to Queens where Michael and Katherine picked her up at the station. From there they drove out together.

They were instructed to meet the real estate agent that Michael spoke with at her office to pick up the key and pay for the rental. Luisa had enough money saved after her share of the tailoring business to pay for the vacation. The woman they met with was cheery and very eager to show them around the area; pointing out the local restaurants and mini markets. When they arrived at the house the first thing Luisa did was open all the windows since it seemed to be muggy inside. There were two bedrooms and Luisa didn't give Michael a hard time about sharing one of the rooms with Katherine. They were both in their 20's and she wasn't playing the mother role with him, which made Michael grateful. Katherine was a very pleasant girl and she was good to Michael. She taught kindergarten at the school down the block from the Bartoloni's house. He ran into her one day at the local deli when he called in sick for work. She was there picking up lunch for herself while Michael picked up his cup of chicken noodle soup. They got to talking and she fell for Michael's charm, and he fell for her sense of humor. It was all uphill from there. They were inseparable.

After unpacking everything, Luisa yelled out that she was going to take a walk on the beach and check out the water. It was so beautiful and peaceful just walking on the sand listening to the ocean churning. She knew that for the rest of her stay there she would try and spend as much time taking walks on the beach after dinner.

The second night, Luisa decided to make dinner for everyone. She walked to the market and purchased some pasta and vegetables to make a fresh meal. On the way out towards the house she noticed a liquor store and picked up a couple of bottles of wine as well. Why not? It was a vacation after all.

That evening, Luisa turned on the radio in the kitchen and opened up a bottle of wine while she started to cook. Michael and Katherine had gone for a walk on the beach. She put the fan in the kitchen, between the stove and the hot, humid air it was overly hot inside. She decided after this meal they were going to have to stick to using the barbeque or heading out to the air-conditioned restaurants. She was having a good time even though she was alone and started dancing to the music while sipping her wine and chopping up some garlic.

After finishing a glass of wine she heard the front door open and Michael calling out to her, "Luisa! Where are you!"

"I'm in the kitchen, is everything alright?" Luisa turned suddenly and saw Michael and Katherine standing behind her with huge smiles on their faces.

"Ok, let me in on the secret," she said.

Katherine put her hand out to show Luisa that she was wearing a diamond ring. It was a small diamond but the meaning was enough to make Luisa scream for joy.

"She said yes!" Michael said, turning to Katherine and embracing her.

"Come over here you two! Oh I'm so happy! I can't believe it, you are all grown up Michael! Congratulations to you both. Welcome to the family Katherine." She gave her a big hug and kiss and then looked at Michael and put her hands on his face. "Tanti auguri." She then kissed both cheeks. "It's a good thing I bought wine, let's celebrate!"

The rest of the vacation was wonderful and relaxing for Luisa. It was just what she needed to get her mind off of Samuel.

Luisa took a bus back to school, and decided to take some summer classes to keep her occupied. There were times, of course, that she had too much time to think. Summer was much less quieter than the usual semesters. Mitchell had not been there and she found that she missed her conversations with him. His witty comments always kept her laughing. She hoped the summer would go fast enough so that once again she would see her friend.

One night Luisa sat out on the big lawn just looking out over the green hills. It was her favorite time of day—dusk. It looked like nighttime below and daytime above but without the bright sun. It was so beautiful. She thought of Michael and how he was going to marry Katherine. Before she knew it, he too would have children and grow old one day. Would she still be around to witness it? How long was her time here on this earth? The thought of watching him grow old and pass away was depressing. She got up and went to the cafeteria. There she bought herself a brownie and headed to the library for a copy of *Pride and Prejudice*. It was the last book Lorenzo had bought for her as a gift. It was also the first book she read in English. She took it back to her room and stayed up reading for two hours until falling asleep. She woke the next morning finding the book on the floor next to her, and an empty brownie wrapper crushed beneath it.

***

It was about a week after everyone was settled in that Mitchell asked Luisa if she would like to join him with some of his friends at a party in the dorms.

"Oh come on, who cares how old you are? You're allowed to have fun too." Mitchell was excited to get invited to the party, but felt

73

bad for Luisa. He noticed that she rarely hung out with anyone after class, and even rarer still didn't seem to have any other friends. Luisa started to hang out with Mitchell and his other friends, but she hung back often so that she didn't affect what little reputation Mitchell had.

"Mitchell, come on now, I'm too old for that. Besides, I want you to go and start a conversation with that Barbara girl. I told you I saw her looking at you the other day in the cafeteria. She will be there, right?"

Mitchell shook his head and turned red. "I don't know. I highly doubt she looked at me unless she was telling her friends what a dork I was. If you don't want to go fine, but don't let me hear how bored you were tonight."

"Are you kidding me? I found out in the TV guide that 'Casablanca' is on tonight. I can't wait to sit home with some ice cream and watch it!" She winked at Mitchell. "Trust me, when you get to my age, that is fun to do."

Mitchell looked at her like she was out of her mind. "Well, let's hope I don't get old fast! Talk to you tomorrow."

"Mitchell," Luisa said. "Promise me you won't drink too much, ok? Be careful."

"Yes, mother." Mitchell responded sarcastically.

Chapter 13

Michael and Katherine decided to get married the following summer. Katherine always wanted to be married in July, even though her mother warned her of how uncomfortable she would be in a wedding gown in the hottest month of the year. She didn't care.

Some of the family flew in from California for the wedding. Giuseppe was there along with Michael's parents and siblings. Everyone was happy to see the lifestyle Luisa and Michael were living. Mr. & Mrs. Bartoloni insisted that they stay at his house. The apartment on the top was vacant for a few months with a new tenant starting in September. There seemed to be a big celebration each night they stayed. Giuseppe and Michael's parents stayed up late with the Bartoloni's drinking and laughing. Michael swore he heard dancing from the floor above him one night. Luisa stayed with Michael in their original apartment, while Katherine stayed with her family. Once Michael and Katherine were married they would both be living there together and Luisa was going to stay in the vacant apartment until she headed back to school.

One evening, Giuseppe retired earlier than the rest and headed to bed. Luisa helped him up the stairs. As she turned to leave Giuseppe asked Luisa to sit down on the couch for a bit.

He looked at her and smiled. "It's hard to imagine that I am your son. All I seem to be is an old man. Not good for much lately, eh?"

"Giuseppe, I don't know how I would have gotten through this without you. I never thought it would last this long. I can't tell you how hard it is for me to see you getting older. Your father would be so proud of you and how well you took care of the vineyard. Your sons will do just as good a job having such a wonderful teacher. I was thinking of visiting during the spring break and staying on the vineyard next summer. What do you think?" Luisa knew that Giuseppe's time was running out. She wanted to be around the family again and even considered taking a break from college. She could always return when her time on the vineyard wasn't needed any longer.

Giuseppe smiled. "That would be nice Luisa. I will make sure you return to school that fall though." He pointed his finger sternly at her. "You have taken care of us all for so long already. Who else gets the gift of having their mother around with them until they are old like

75

me? Ah, we have plenty of family helping out. You did your time, Luisa."

"But Giuseppe, it's not just to take care of you which, yes, I would do that too. I just...I just want to be around my children. That's all."

He saw in her eyes what she was thinking. She wanted to be there for when they passed away. Mario and Maria were also elderly. She went back to California only once since leaving and was starting to feel guilty for not staying with them until the end.

"It's always a pleasure having you back at home. Whatever you decide to do I will support you. For now, I must go to bed. It's a big day tomorrow. If I don't go to sleep now I won't last the afternoon!" He got up from the couch and headed to the bedroom.

Luisa sat there thinking how unbelievable everything had been. She should not be sitting on that couch and she should not be attending her great-grandson's wedding in better shape than the parents of the groom. It was impossible and yet she was the lucky one to witness it all. She just hoped that Lorenzo was watching from above as well.

Chapter 14

Everyone got up early to get ready for the wedding. Luisa made sure that all the men's suits fit well and then she headed over to Katherine's house where she was getting ready with her bridesmaids. Katherine had asked Luisa to make the dresses for the bridal party. One night all the women got together and designed the dress. When Luisa presented the finished product to them they were all extremely satisfied with the result. Luisa really was talented.

The church was not far from the house and the reception was to be held at a hall in the city. Katherine's family took care of all the arrangements. The ceremony turned out to be just as lovely as the weather that day. Everything was perfect and Luisa was so grateful to be part of it.

After the church and some pictures, they all headed into the city for the reception. There were two limos that followed each other. Everyone was in a great mood and ready to party as they headed out of the car. The girls were just about to enter the hall when Luisa realized she left her bouquet in the car.

"Oh! My flowers! I'll be right back."

"Luisa hurry the limo is going to pull away!" Katherine's sister shouted.

She made it in time and got her flowers; Luisa and the limo driver laughed together about how bad it would be if she forgot them altogether. Just as she turned to head back to the hall she bumped into someone. It was a man and a woman walking together.

"Oh my goodness, I'm so sorry." She looked up and there was Samuel looking at her in disbelief.

"Luisa?"

"Samuel! Hi, how are you? Ah, Michael is, Michael just got married and…"

He cut her off, "How have you been? You look wonderful."

Luisa smiled shyly looking over at the woman with Samuel.

"I'm sorry. Luisa this is Katie, Katie this is Luisa."

Luisa put her hand out. "Pleased to meet you, Katie," she said, smiling. She turned to Samuel. "I really must get going; they are all waiting for me. It was nice to see you."

She hurried to the front entrance of the hall. When she got inside she stood still trying to catch her breath. Never did she expect to see Samuel. Of all the streets he could have been walking on why the one she was at? The woman with Samuel looked like a model as well. Just what she needed to see. She had finally gotten Samuel out of her head with all the wedding preparations keeping her busy. She decided that she wasn't going to let it ruin her evening. Today was Michael's day and Giuseppe was here. She was going to enjoy it to the fullest. She didn't need Samuel. Although she quickly imagined him being there with her at the wedding. But forced the thought out of her head.

"There you are! They want to take a family picture, come on!" Michael was at the end of the hallway. She wasn't going to tell him what just happened. No need to, he had enough on his mind now. Michael was a little worried about taking care of Katherine. He hoped that he made enough money to support her. She had already mentioned buying a house one day and the pressure was on. He was determined to work his way up the ladder at the paper, so all it did was motivate him.

The wedding turned out to be a lot of fun for everyone. Luisa booked a hotel for Michael and his new wife close to the airport. The next day, they were leaving for Sicily. Giuseppe had given them the trip as a wedding present.

The following morning, Luisa slept in later than usual. It was a long night and she was exhausted. Giuseppe and the family took a cab back to the airport that afternoon. It was sad to see everyone leaving. She had so enjoyed seeing everyone together again and part of her missed her days on the vineyard. She knew, however, those days were long gone and she admitted to liking her new life.

That evening, she decided to walk around the corner and get a slice of pizza to bring back to the apartment. She had been eating a ton of food in the last week and wanted something small. On her way out, as she started to head down the street, someone called her name. "Luisa?"

She looked up and it was Samuel.

Not again, she thought.

"Samuel. Hi. What brings you here?"

He looked over her shoulder towards the apartment. Luisa turned and looked to see Mrs. Bartoloni looking through the door and closing it suddenly after seeing Luisa turn around.

"I see," she said.

"I'm sorry to bother you. It's just when I saw you the other day...you looked so beautiful. Not that you never have it's just I realized how much I missed you. Luisa I've been thinking a lot about you. I wasn't sure how long you were staying. I assumed you would head back to California with the rest of the family but when I called the Bartoloni's, they told me you would be here for a few more weeks. I hope it's ok that I stopped by." He looked so desperate; not as confident of a man as she remembered. Although he still was handsome as ever.

"Samuel, I don't know if that's such a great idea." She saw the disappointment in his eyes and it tore at her heart. He suddenly relaxed and looked up to the sky. She had hoped it wasn't because he didn't want to shed any tears.

"Were you headed anywhere right now?" He was more casual with her now.

"I was going to grab a slice of pizza actually." She thought for a moment. "Would you care to join me?"

He suddenly smiled. "Yeah, that would be great."

They both walked around the block together. It was strange not to hold his arm as she used to when they walked together. It was a bit awkward and she wasn't sure what to do with her arms so she just folded them as she walked.

"So how have you been Samuel? Are you still doing the same work?"

He laughed. "Of course, did you think I started to make suits perhaps?"

She didn't find it to be as funny.

"Sorry," he said. "I wasn't trying to be a jerk."

"Oh, it's alright. It was a stupid question." She now wished he hadn't shown up.

When they entered the pizzeria, they were greeted by Carlo. "Luisa, che se dice? Eh, Samuel. Good to see you." He put his hand out to shake Samuel's hand.

"Carlo, how are you. I sure missed your pizza that's for sure." They shook hands.

They ordered their food and sat down at a bench nearby.

Samuel started the conversation first this time. "So how is California doing?"

She was grateful to see the Bartoloni's did not tell him about her going back to school. She just needed to tell them tonight to keep their mouths shut the next time Samuel decided to call again.

"Good. Things are good. The same really."

It was quiet again. They were both grateful for Carlo's interruption that their food was up.

Samuel got up and brought it to their table.

"Thank you." Luisa took the oregano and put it by Samuel knowing he liked that on his pizza.

"You see, that is why you are not like all the other women out there, Luisa. You know how to take care of me." He laughed.

"Are you telling me that other women don't take care of you? Oh come now, I find that hard to believe." She was teasing him.

"Not like you." He took a bite of his pizza and shook his head continuing to talk, even with a mouthful. "You know me. You know what I like and you think of others before thinking about yourself. It's just the way you are."

"Well, I don't know about that. I think of myself all the time."

"Yes! And that's why you are so put together. You are a gem Luisa. A perfect catch. You know, kid," he put his pizza down and leaned forward, "I really missed you."

She looked at him. "Well it didn't look that way yesterday. I'm sure you weren't thinking of me when you picked up that beautiful blond for the evening." Some more teasing on her end.

"Hey now, that's not fair. I haven't seen you in forever. I just needed a night out that's all. She means nothing. She has no personality. No backbone. She just wants my money."

They both laughed.

"How about you. You seeing anyone?" He tried to keep his voice nonchalant, but she could hear the fear in his voice.

"Me? No, I'm not seeing anyone. Well, wait a minute. There *is* someone. He is well over ten years younger than I am, but he's a doll."

Samuel looked up all wide-eyed. "Ten years younger? What's that about?"

She laughed. "Ok, you got me. I went back to school. It keeps me busy." She figured he didn't need to know where it was she was going. There are schools in California as well. "This young boy, well he's just my friend. I was only joking."

"Listen, a beautiful woman like yourself and trust me, he's hoping it will become more than friends. Shall I call you Mrs. Robinson?" He laughed and raised his eyebrows.

"You're silly. Trust me, Mitchell is on the nerdy side. He only talks to me because he is too scared to talk to any other girl."

"School, huh? What are you taking up besides space?"

"Space?" She looked puzzled.

"Space. You know, taking up space, room? Oh forget it." He took another bite.

"Oh!" She finally understood his little joke. "Well, I am going to be a teacher one day. At least I hope to be."

He seemed impressed. "A teacher! That's great. I wouldn't mind being a student in *your* class!" he said, smiling.

Luisa missed Samuel and how fun he could be. It was too bad things couldn't have worked out. She even started to wonder if she had made a mistake leaving him. But wasn't sure how he would react over the years of her condition. She couldn't take the chance.

"So what do ya say? Can I see you again before you head back to California? I assume you are going back for fall semester right?"

Luisa wasn't sure how to answer. She didn't think it was a good idea to see him again. She knew how irresistible he could be.

"I don't know. Won't it make it harder to say goodbye?" She looked at him now in a different teasing kind of way. More sensual this time.

"Well, that's a risk I'm willing to take, my dear." He took her hand in his catching her off guard.

"I'm really tired from last night. I think I'll head back now."

They cleaned their trays and said goodnight to Carlo.

Walking back to the apartment, he asked, "So, is that a yes or a no? About getting together again? What about dinner one night?"

She kept looking down. This time they walked much closer together. Not holding hands or anything, but their arms touched as they walked, they felt much less awkward than before.

Luisa looked up and shook her head because she couldn't believe what she was about to say. She tried to hide her smile. "Sure, ok."

Samuel was thrilled. He put his arm around her shoulders, squeezing gently. "Great. I'll pick you up at 6:00 Saturday. How's that sound?"

"Great."

My car is here, so...I'll see you then?" The awkwardness was back. Do they give each other a kiss goodnight or not? He bent down and kissed her cheek. That seemed to be appropriate enough.

"Goodnight," she said.

"Goodnight, Luisa." He turned towards the car but then back around again. "Hey, it was great to see you again."

"Yes, it was nice." She smiled.

As she got to the front door she took her key out. Before she could even put it in the door, it opened. It was Mrs. Bartoloni. "Ciao cara. So, how was your pizza?"

Luisa gave her a dirty look. "That was pretty sneaky of you!" She playfully pinched the older woman on her arm.

"Ooch!" Mrs. Bartoloni laughed. "Luisa, he loves you! He's a good man who'd take good care of you. You non have to be a teacher. You non need a job if you marry him."

"Marry? Nobody is marrying anyone. Goodnight!" She headed downstairs. Tomorrow she would move her clothes to the upstairs

81

apartment. Right now she needed to sleep. The problem was she couldn't. All she thought about was Samuel. Was Mrs. Bartoloni right? Life could be so easy with Samuel. She really enjoyed spending time with him. She missed the companionship of a man lately.

Being surrounded by college students was starting to get to her. They were so different then she was. But she knew that even if she did have a life with Samuel she still needed to be able to have a career of her own if things went bad. She couldn't always rely on others. She received payments from Giuseppe for her share of the vineyard every month. They did so well it was more than enough. She was very wise with her money and saved most of it. She only spent what was needed to survive really. She knew, however, that she needed *something* in her life and teaching is what she wanted that *something* to be.

Chapter 15

That Saturday, she spent the morning at the hair salon. She figured she might as well look her best for Samuel. Why not? That makes two weeks in a row she splurged on her looks. It felt nice after all.

On her way back home, The Bartoloni's were outside gardening. When they saw that she had her hair done they both smiled and raised their eyebrows knowingly.

"Oh, be quiet," she said as she walked right past them.

She told Samuel she would meet him out front at 6:00. She didn't want him to ring the doorbell. She told the Bartoloni's they were headed out at 7:00 instead, this way they would not be there at the door waiting. She was getting tired of their remarks. She stood outside and saw Samuel's car pulling up. He was hardly able to stop when she opened the door and got in.

"Jeeze Luise!" Michael had passed that saying on to everyone. "At least let me stop the car lady!"

"Oh just start driving, come on now. Hurry up." Luisa waved her hands motioning him to keep driving.

"I hope you got enough at the bank at least. Are the cops going to start following us?"

She looked at him confused. "What are you talking about?"

He looked at her. "Oh forget it. You used to enjoy my little jokes. It just seemed like you robbed a bank and I was your getaway car."

"Oh!" she laughed, "You're cute."

"Cute. That's what I've become? I was hoping to hear something more like 'distinguished'"

"Well, I like cute. When you start getting grey hair I will call you distinguished, but for now you are cute." She looked over and smiled at him.

They headed into the city. To her surprise he pulled up to the same restaurant they had gone on their first date together.

"Oh, this place looks familiar," she said.

"Is that ok? I thought it would be nice to come back and visit. If you're not comfortable we could go someplace else."

"Oh no, I love it here. Don't be silly."

83

He was glad to hear that. Deep down he hoped that he could win her over again. After Luisa left, Samuel wasn't himself. Not even his old self. The party man inside of him shut down. He realized after being with her he wanted more to life and no matter how many dates he went on he just couldn't find it with anyone else. He couldn't tease other women like he teased Luisa. He actually loved that she didn't understand some of his jokes. He thought it was cute. There were even times he thought about heading to California to go after her. He wasn't sure if the Bartoloni's would give him her address, but another part of him knew they would probably take him there themselves.

They headed inside and sat at the same table they sat at on their first date. She had to laugh.

"Did you plan all of this?" She sat down.

"Well, as much as I would like to say it's a coincidence, I can't."

"Do you think they will have the same items on the menu?" The waiter took her napkin off the table and handed it to her. She placed it on her lap.

"I hope so but, as much as I love the food here I would trade it in a second for a meal from you. You are still the best cook in town, baby."

"You should have told me, I would have cooked for you tonight instead."

He put the wine list down. "Wait, are you telling me I could've had a night at your place? Boy, I screwed up again."

She laughed, "Well, when you put it that way, forget it."

"The night is still young, sweet-cheeks." He winked at her.

He ordered a bottle of wine. Moments later the waiter brought it over and opened it, pouring some in Samuel's glass. Samuel took the glass and handed it to Luisa. "Here you taste it this time." He looked at the waiter. "She's the real wine expert. She grew up on a vineyard you know."

Luisa gave him a look of annoyance. "Samuel!" She pushed the glass back to him. "Don't be silly, you ordered it, you taste it."

Samuel laughed, "Ok." He swirled the wine, took a sip, then nodded to the waiter.

She realized that something must have changed for him to do such a thing. Samuel had to always be in charge, especially when it came to women. It seemed he softened up a bit. That pleased Luisa.

"So what else have you been up to?" He was curious about her life without him in it. "Are you still making suits?"

She laughed. "Nobody wears suits on a vineyard. There is no need."

"I still think you made a mistake giving up that business. When you are good at something you should stick to it." The businessman was back.

"Well, maybe one day I will be good at teaching and helping children."

"I'm sure you will. You seem to be good at everything, Luisa." He looked at her with admiration. "You know, there are schools here too. You don't have to go to school in California. I would get to see you more often if you moved back here."

Luisa was worried this is where the night would take them. Back to getting together in a relationship. As much as she would like to be with Samuel, again, how could she explain to him in ten years what's going on. Sure, she figured she could get another ten years looking the same, but then what? She falls deeper in love and now it's going on twenty years. She was sure at that point he would think something was strange. It wasn't worth the heartache. It had been hard enough to deal with watching Lorenzo grow old and pass away; and now she'd have to watch her children too. She didn't want to get attached again like that. She never got the opportunity to know Giovanni as much as she wished she had. Another loss would be more of a shove in her face that she is going to be on this road alone for a very long time. She figured it was best to do it alone. How much more could she take? Not to mention it wouldn't be fair to Samuel. Although something tells her that having a young wife forever wouldn't be a bad deal, especially for a man like him. But it would be a lie.

"Samuel, my family needs me now, I have to stay in California."

"What happened with us? I mean really. Did I do something to scare you away? Was it the marriage proposal? Listen, I'm not asking for all of that again. I just really miss your company. That's all." He was being as sincere as he can.

She smiled. "I missed you too. I really did. It's nice being here with you again. The thing is, for reasons I can't really explain, it just will not work out. Samuel, I'm sorry but in a way I wish my life was different. This has absolutely nothing to do with you. You are an amazing man and quite frankly an amazing catch. I just can't be in a relationship. Not with you, not with anyone."

Confusion blanketed his face. "That just doesn't make sense to me. Luisa you are the most old-fashioned woman I have ever met. It just seems you of all people would want to be married with children."

She winced. If he only knew she had already been there, done that. She was married for many years and raised three children. Now they were aging, dying.

Noticing her reaction Samuel reached across the table in apology. "Luisa, oh my gosh. I'm so sorry. It never occurred to me. Are you not able to have children?"

Luisa didn't expect him to say that at all but thinking quickly she realized that it was a good excuse. "Oh Samuel. I really would rather not discuss it." She figured she would leave it to his imagination. This way she didn't have to lie.

He took her hand on the table and squeezed. "I don't care about that Luisa. I wasn't even sure if I ever wanted kids to be honest. I just want to be with you."

"Samuel, please. Can we just enjoy our time together tonight and not talk about anything else?" She seemed desperate now.

He saw she was getting upset and agreed with her. "I'm sorry. Yes, you are right, we were having such a good time. I'll keep my big mouth shut." He laughed.

The night ended and she tried her best to be quiet when she arrived at home so as not to wake up her nosey neighbors. It was hard for her to fall asleep that night. She wondered about her life and how much longer she could be spending it alone. It really did not seem flattering to her. Even though she had her life with Lorenzo, she also had a long life alone. She realized the importance of a companion. Someone who would always be there with you. Someone you could talk to about your day right before going to sleep every night. Knowing that someone would be there for you when you were sad. Sure, she had friends that she could talk to, but it wasn't the same. Even Sara had become too busy with her own family to spend much time with Luisa. Michael was busy with Katherine now, her family was across the country, and there was only a year left of school and then Mitchell would be gone too.

Would it be so horrible to enjoy some of her years with Samuel?

Some relationships don't work out anyway, she thought.

Today, people didn't seem to stick together like they did during her times. There was no such thing as divorce back then, but now—it happened all the time. And right now, Samuel would take whatever he could. She wouldn't have to marry him. She couldn't do that anyway. Why not live the way that this generation did? Everyone seemed so free now. It made her sad but at the same time, she thought why not take advantage of this adventure?

She decided that the next time she saw Samuel she was going to tell him that she would like to have another shot at their relationship. She could always take classes closer by and this way she would be closer to Michael. She was tired of always running away.

The next afternoon Samuel called her and asked if she wanted to come by his apartment that evening and they could cook a meal together. It was perfect. She would tell him during dinner. She offered to pick up the groceries and he had more than enough wine at his apartment. She was going to take the train in to meet him and he just laughed at her and said he would get her at 5:30.

They decided to make veal cutlets with linguini in white clam sauce. He helped her cook the entire time.

"Look at you. You look like you know what you are doing." She teased him.

"Listen, after eating your meals I couldn't go back to take out every night. I had to learn to cook *something*! You were a good teacher."

"See I told you I would be a good teacher one day." She bumped hips with him.

They had music playing in the background and candles all around. It was the perfect atmosphere and she was happy with her decision to try and work things out with Samuel.

They finally sat down to eat. The table was set with more candles and the music turned lower and switched to opera.

They weren't even halfway through and Samuel seemed very anxious to tell her something. "I have to tell you something. I invited you here to tell you and I was going to wait until dessert but I just can't hold it in any longer."

Luisa was very curious and was hoping to share her news with him during dessert as she could wait a little longer. "Sure, what is it?"

"Well, for the last year now we have been working on expanding our company. Worldwide. Everything finally came to a close and we have an office opening in Paris."

"Paris! Oh how exciting!" Luisa couldn't believe that she had spent all these years on this earth and she never traveled anywhere.

"I will be the one heading over there to run things for now." He was leaning on the table and she saw he was biting his lip after he said that. He was nervous and she could see.

"Samuel that's wonderful. Is this something you want to do?" She suddenly realized that her news would not fit in with his plans and was so grateful that she didn't mention it before he had. She had no right to be upset or sad. After all, she left him and he had to move on with his life. Part of her was jealous and even a larger part of her was sad that he would be living so far away now.

"Luisa, I knew about this and I didn't bring it up right away because I figured why bother. I mean you will be heading back to California and I still had a month to get things together. I'm still working on finding an apartment. I've been back and forth for meetings to finalize everything over the year. My next trip there will be a one way ticket, for now at least."

"Well, I'm really happy for you Samuel. You seem excited about this. Do you speak any French?" She managed a smile, even though inside she was hurting.

"Just a little, enough to get me by." He leaned closer to her, she could see by the expression on his face he was about to question her on something. "Hey, so...do you think by any chance, maybe you would want to come with me?" He was so frightened to ask her this. After their conversation at the restaurant the other night she made it clear that she did not want to discuss their future together. He wasn't sure if just bringing it up would cause her to leave, but he had to take the chance.

Looking at her, he could see tears well up in her eyes. "Luisa, I'm sorry. I know I shouldn't have - "

"Samuel, you have no idea what you just did. You somehow managed to turn what I was going to talk to *you* about into something even more spectacular."

He looked confused, but a smirk started to form at the edges of his mouth. "Wait, does this mean you will think about it?"

"I don't need time to think about it. I came tonight to tell you that I would like to give us a shot again. But never did I think we could be doing it in Paris! I've never been there before!" She was so excited at the very thought.

He got up from his chair and lifted her out of hers. They kissed and he whisked her up in his arms and took her to the bedroom.

Chapter 16

Luisa picked up Michael and Katherine at the airport from their honeymoon. They had a wonderful time and were more in love than ever before.

"Buon giorno!" Luisa gave them both a big hug. "So, how was it?"

"Amazing!" Katherine squealed. She babbled about their trip the whole way home. Luisa decided she would tell Michael about Samuel and Paris when the time was right. She wanted to let them settle in first. She had moved all of her stuff to the upstairs apartment and filled their kitchen with food so they would be all set once they arrived home.

"Michael?" Luisa asked, tugging on his shirt. He turned to her, smiling. "After dinner do you mind stopping by to speak with me about something?"

"Of course. Is everything alright?" he asked, concerned.

"Yes, yes of course!" She laughed.

They agreed to have coffee up at her apartment that night. She didn't want to impose on them with dinner and knew as newlyweds they should be alone.

Later that night Michael and Katherine came upstairs with a few souvenirs for Luisa from Sicily. He handed her a miniature horse and carriage—a symbol of Sicilian culture.

"As if you don't have enough of these right?" Michael laughed.

"Aw, that was sweet. Thank you."

"So, what's been going on since we were away? Did I miss anything exciting? Did everyone get back to California ok?"

"Yes, and we all had a wonderful time at the wedding. It was so much fun!" Luisa was happy to tell them all about it but really wanted to get right to her main reason for bringing them up there. She had to tell them about Samuel.

"Ok so, I didn't tell you this because it was your day and no need for me to complain or anything but the day of your wedding I bumped into Samuel outside of the wedding hall."

"Really? Oh my gosh, how was that? Awkward I bet." Michael's eyebrows were raised.

"Well considering he was with a beautiful woman, sure."

89

"Oh no, I'm sorry Luisa, that had to hurt. Are you ok?" Katherine said, placing a hand on top of Luisa's. Katherine was a very sweet girl, always wanting to help.

Luisa waved her hand as if it meant nothing. "Oh sure, I'm fine. I mean it was strange at first, sure. And of course I thought about him all night after the wedding, which was hard but the next day he showed up out front waiting for me."

"Let me guess, the Bartoloni's?" Michael knew how much they adored Samuel and was upset that Luisa did not marry him.

She laughed. "You guessed it! Anyway, we ended up getting a quick bite."

Michael sat forward on the couch looking at her suspiciously. "And...?"

"Well, one thing led to another and we are going to try to give it another shot."

"Really? Way to go Sammy! I always liked him, you know that. But I thought you couldn't be together because of your 'situation.'" He put his fingers up to make quotes in the air.

She looked at Katherine knowing that she must not have known what she was talking about.

Michael said, "It's ok. I told her while we were in Sicily. Don't get mad, she's not going to say a word. Besides she just thinks we all have mental issues or something and doesn't believe it anyway."

Katherine hit Michael in the arm. "Michael!"

"What? It's the truth!"

Katherine looked at Luisa who's eyes grew wide. "Don't listen to him—"

Luisa cut her off and laughed. "It's ok. Better that way probably! Anyway, that's not everything."

"You're getting married?" Michael demanded, enthusiastically.

"No! I'm not and keep it down, that's the last thing I need the Bartoloni's to hear!" Luisa hit his arm.

"Ok, can everyone stop hitting me!" Michael said, annoyed.

"I'm going to move to Paris with him. I don't know how long. He is supposed to be there for a year at least. I figure why not, right?" She looked concerned at Michael. One minute she was thinking that it would be great to be closer to Michael and Katherine and the next minute she was moving farther away.

"Wow! Paris, huh? That's far." Michael was looking down, worried about Luisa being that far all alone.

Katherine cut him off. "But oh my God so exciting!" She got up and hugged Luisa. "I'm so happy for you. Luisa you deserve this. I don't know why you ever left him. He could take care of you and he clearly loves you so much. I'm so jealous!"

"Really?" Michael looked at Katherine. "Thanks a lot!"

Both women laughed.

"So when do you leave?" Katherine asked.

"A little over a week. I already settled things with school. I will return again, I just don't know exactly when."

"Life is too short right?" He looked at her smiling.

"Very funny," Luisa said.

****

The day had come for Samuel and Luisa to head to Paris. They were staying at a hotel until they found a place to settle in. It was hard saying goodbye to Michael but she told him that she would not be staying forever.

"A year goes very fast in my eyes remember? And we'll try to come back for Christmas," she told him.

Michael seemed sad. "I worry Luisa, I know grandpa is not happy about this."

"He's fine. It doesn't matter anyway, he has no choice. I'm going. I can take care of myself and I have Samuel."

"Who doesn't know about your condition. What if something were to happen?"

"It won't. If it does then I come straight home, I promise." Luisa kissed Michael on the cheek. "Take care of that wife of yours now. I'm not your responsibility anymore, love."

The flight wasn't as bad as she had expected. She made sure to bring a book with her to read. Samuel kept telling her she should get some rest but she couldn't sleep at all. She was too excited.

When they finally arrived, she was even more energetic and couldn't wait to see the famed streets of Paris. Samuel was not to start working for another week. He took the time to get settled with Luisa and see some sights. He convinced Luisa not to worry about work since the apartment was getting paid through the company. He wanted her to enjoy her time there and relax. She had no problem doing that.

The hotel was perfect for them. He upgraded the room so that they had a living area and enough space to move around since he wasn't sure how long it would take to find a place to live. Luisa's only complaint was that there was no kitchen. Living in the hotel would not work out for very long.

"Oh, check this out!" Samuel exclaimed, taking Luisa's hand and pulling her to the balcony doors. As they stepped out Luisa looked to her right, and to her amazement, in front of her stood the Eiffel Tower.

"Oh my God! It's so beautiful!" She felt like she had just stepped into a movie scene and she was playing the main role.

"I'm guessing at night will be even better." Samuel pulled her back into the room. "Now, I have better business to take care of while we are here. After all, we *are* in Paris, the city of love."

"I believe it's the city of lights." She corrected him.

"I like my way better." He kissed her on the lips.

They ordered room service for lunch and ended up falling asleep for a couple of hours. The long flight back finally caught up to them.

"What do you say? Wanna head out and find a nice place to eat? Maybe walk over to the tower after?"

"Sounds like a plan to me. Casual tonight?" She didn't unpack any of her stuff yet and was looking at the suitcase wondering what she would wear.

"Yes, tonight is casual. Tomorrow night I will take you to the best restaurant in town, how about that?" He pulled her closer to him.

"Sounds perfect." She kissed him again.

After showering and getting ready, she waited out by the front door for Samuel. He was talking to the concierge to book a nice restaurant for the next evening. She looked around still amazed that she was there in Paris. What took her so long? All those years on the vineyard after Lorenzo was gone. Why didn't she head back to Europe instead? She figured it had to do with Giuseppe not wanting her to be alone. I guess in a way it was good. She managed to grow independent in New York with the help of Michael.

Samuel came out. "Ready to roll?"

They walked arm in arm through the streets looking for a restaurant to eat at. She loved that everyone was eating outside at the café's and they chose one to dine in.

The waiter came over speaking in French. She realized she could figure out what it was he was saying. It sounded somewhat like Italian only a lot sexier.

Samuel asked if he spoke English and instantly the waiter spoke their language.

The meal was just what they needed and they headed towards The Eiffel Tower. Paris was so romantic at night all lit up.

"I told you it was the city of lights," Luisa said.

"I still like the city of love better." He nibbled her ear.

They arrived at the tower with all the other tourists.

"It's so amazing isn't it. I mean it's so big. What a great symbol. You see pictures in books but it's nothing like it is in person."

"Come on, we need to get under it. It's bad luck if you don't kiss under The Eiffel Tower."

"Oh, any excuse for a kiss."

"That's right baby and don't forget it." He kissed the top of her head.

The night turned out perfect and they walked around the neighborhood until they were tired and went back to the hotel. The next few days they did the popular sights of Paris. The Louvre, Notre Dame and of course did some shopping. They took a couple of days to look at some apartments as well. They were exceptional places. She told Samuel he needed to decide which one since she really couldn't make a decision. They were to move in a week. The place he chose was furnished already which turned out to be perfect for them. He wasn't sure how long he would be staying there.

Once Samuel started going to work and they had moved into their apartment, Luisa felt she had to try and figure out a routine for herself. She went walking every morning, which seemed more like a treat than a chore since the streets and shops were all beautiful. She would go to different sections of Paris and walk around there. She was becoming pretty familiar with the entire area. Sometimes she would come across what looked like a perfect romantic restaurant. She would walk in and make a reservation and ask for a card so she had the address to return with Samuel.

Everything was really turning out to be nice for her. She was even picking up some of the language. One day, on one of her walks she passed an antique shop and after looking in the window for what seemed too long, she decided to walk in. Even though they talked about not decorating the apartment so much with their own stuff, she sometimes would buy little things here and there although Samuel was worried about leaving it behind by accident.

She walked toward the back of the store and everything seemed really beautiful although sadly very expensive as well. There were four paintings hung up on the wall. One she saw and fell in love with instantly. It was the exact scene that she witnessed with Samuel the first night they arrived in Paris. It was of The Eiffel Tower and the River Seine all lit up at night.

She saw a man standing in the back and motioned for him to come over to her. "Excuse…" She realized she should ask in French. "Pardon?"

"Madam speaks English?" The man had a heavy accent but was able to speak English, which made things easier for her.

"Yes, I do thank you. Can you tell me how much this painting is?"

"That one in American money, one thousand and two hundred dollars."

"Oh wow." Luisa was surprised at how much and put her hand to her mouth pondering if it was worth it.

"Madam, eh well known painter."

"I see, well thank you. Perhaps I will be back."

"Eh." The man knew she wouldn't and shrugged his shoulders walking towards the back of the store again.

It was too bad, she thought about buying the painting for a memory of their trip to Paris but felt it was too much money to spend right now. Although, as she got back to the apartment she thought even more about the painting. She realized that she had plenty of money of her own so what was the big deal? Why not get something she enjoyed? She told Samuel about the painting and he said he would go with her that weekend to purchase it. She very well couldn't carry it on her own.

That weekend she took him back to the same store where the painting was. At first she had trouble finding it. They ended up stopping for lunch at one point because she appeared to be lost but would never admit that to Samuel.

He teased her about it, he could see the worry in her face that she wouldn't find the store again. "Hey, the important thing is we had one of the best lunches here."

"I know where it is Samuel. I just thought maybe you would like to stop and eat first is all."

Eventually they found the store. Turns out they had passed the corner a few times only headed in the wrong direction.

They walked inside and Luisa immediately spotted the man she spoke with the other day. "Ah, Monsieur! Bonjour!"

"Oui Madam. Bonjour." He recognized her.

"Can you tell me, the painting that was here the other day…," she was pointing in the same spot and instead of the painting from the other day hanging on the wall was another painting of a café with outdoor seating. "Can you tell me where it is? I would like to purchase it." She smiled at him all excited about her new French find.

"Ah Madam, it is gone. Someone, he bought it yesterday. The paintings here go fast. Perhaps Madam would like another? We have many to choose from?" He waved to the other paintings but she had her heart set on the one.

"No, thank you." Luisa turned to face Samuel and started to walk out.

Samuel put his arm around her shoulders. "I'm sorry sweetie. I know you had your heart set on that one painting. We'll find something else like it."

She was so disappointed but knew it wasn't a reason to be sad. She was in Paris after all. There will be other paintings for her to choose from.

Samuel had been working long hours lately. Some nights he would come home and tell Luisa that they had already ordered in dinner while they worked. She ended up eating dinner most nights alone. Some weekends he even had to go to the office. One night she had enough.

"You know, I am here all alone all day long Samuel. I mean, that is fine and everything but by the time you get home it's almost time for bed! I understand that you are busy but what am I supposed to do with my time alone? I can't even watch TV because I don't understand what anyone is saying. In fact, I don't understand what anyone is saying anywhere! I can't go to a movie, I can't really make friends. What am I supposed to do?"

Samuel was very tired and in no mood for arguing. "Luisa, I just opened the office for Christ's sake. This is important right now. What do you want from me?"

"Your attention would be nice!"

"I don't need this right now." He got up and walked into the bathroom. She heard the shower go on and tried to go in there but he had locked the door.

"You are such an idiot!" She yelled knowing he probably could not hear her over the running water.

They went to bed that night still angry although he kissed her goodnight before falling asleep. She didn't answer and instead pretended to be asleep by the time he was out of the bathroom.

The next morning she woke up after he had left for the office. She sat up realizing how tired he really must be knowing he left so early. She decided to make it up to him for snapping at him the way she did. She prepared his favorite pasta dish and packed it in a container to bring to his office along with some fruit. He never showed her exactly where his office was but he had some cards in his drawer with the new office location on them. She grabbed one and headed down to grab a cab.

She showed the driver the address on the card. It wasn't very far from the apartment and she realized she probably could walk next time. Luisa handed money to the driver and thanked him as she got out of the car.

She pointed to the building before she closed the door asking the driver if that was the correct one.

"Oui." He motioned to go towards the big red door in front of them.

Luisa wasn't sure how she was going to get inside, she started to look around for a buzzer of some sorts and suddenly the door opened and a man came out.

"Oh, pardon," she said.

He saw she was trying to enter and held the door for her before leaving.

It opened up into a courtyard with doors all around. She looked at each door until she came across Samuel's company name on one of them. The door was unlocked so she entered and headed up the stairway.

There were several other doors at the top but again she saw his firm name outside on one of them. The door had been halfway opened so she walked in looking around and saw there were a few desks around with papers all over them and nobody there. It looked like someone had just left because there were filled cups with black coffee. She heard voices down the hall and kept walking towards them. When she got to the end there was another office with a door halfway opened. She looked inside to see Samuel sitting in his chair laughing and looking up at a very attractive woman who was leaning on his desk and facing him. She was laughing as well and definitely way too close to Samuel. What woman would stand right in front of a man while he sat behind his desk. Well, she knew what kind of woman would do that and she did not like it one bit.

Luisa cleared her throat to notify them she was standing there. They both quickly turned around to see who it was and Samuel's face looked like he had seen a ghost.

Luisa walked toward them with no expression. "I brought you lunch, I thought maybe you were sick of ordering in." She placed it down on his desk, looked at him and without moving her head, moved her eyes toward the woman who was standing there silent holding a folder close to her bosom. Luisa then turned and walked towards the door closing her eyes wishing that she could disappear and be outside.

"Luisa, wait." Samuel was coming after her. Just what she didn't want. It was happening all over again. Just like the day in his office when she said good-bye to him the first time. Only now, she was the one hurting. She continued to walk ignoring him the entire time.

"Would you stop walking? What are you doing?" Samuel was getting annoyed.

"No, you go back to your busy work. I can see how much you have to do. I can also see why you chose to stay late and not come home." She started to walk down the stairs.

"What? You have got to be kidding me." Samuel seemed annoyed at the accusation. "Luisa. Luisa! Stop walking and talk to me! What are you doing? You are acting like a child."

She stopped and turned to him. "I have been sitting in that apartment all day and all night. When I'm not sitting there I am walking the streets in another country all alone. I am *always* all alone. You, however, have Miss Frenchie there to keep you company. What do I have? Samuel, I never should have come here with you." She was feeling sick and realized what a mistake it had been to make such a move. She didn't have many classes left to graduate and she threw it all away. She paused it all for a man. Never did she think she would do this. What she should have done is finished school and then move to wherever it was she wanted. She could have seen the world then. She couldn't believe how stupid she had been. Samuel was a player and always would be.

He grabbed her by the shoulders. "Listen to me. There is nobody else in my life I want to be with other than you. Don't you dare stand there and accuse me of anything. I was having a laugh with someone, that is it. I'm sorry that I have not been around enough for you lately. I didn't think this would take so much time to figure out. It's only me and John here and we are up to our asses in work. Excuse me for taking a second to breathe and smile." He let go of her and turned the other way with his hands on his sides. "Thank you for bringing the lunch. It was very sweet of you."

Luisa looked at him confused and hurt. She turned and left without another word.

That night, Samuel came home earlier than he had been lately. She figured he would after the day they had. When he arrived inside Luisa was sitting on the couch. He looked over to her and there on the floor were two big suitcases.

"Are you serious?" He just stood there in shock. "Luisa, I did nothing wrong."

She stood up and walked over to him. "I know." She took his hand in hers. "Samuel I do believe you. It's me. I can't do this anymore. You are busy with the new office and that's fine. Really. It's the way it should be. But, for me, this isn't the way it should be. Paris so far was amazing for me. But it's not home. I have things I need to finish. I can't put my life on hold anymore. Believe it or not, I've been doing too much of that. I need to start doing things I want to do. I really want to finish school and get my degree. Paris was great to visit but it's not my home. I'm so sorry."

Samuel loosened up after seeing that she believed he did no wrong. He put his arms around her. "Jeeze Luise. I can't seem to hold on to you can I?"

"You'll do just fine without me."

"Are you kidding? Now I have to eat French food every night. I was looking forward to your good homemade Italian food every night."

She laughed, "Well maybe if you were here to eat it more often…"

"Yeah, yeah. I know. I'm sorry."

"It's ok. We tried." They continued to hug.

"When are you leaving?"

"First thing in the morning."

"So I still have you for one more night?"

"Did you want to go out to eat?"

"No, we are staying in tonight."

Chapter 17

Luisa had called Michael to let him know what was going on and asked if he could pick her up at the airport. He met her at the gate.

"I'm really sorry, Luisa." Michael was genuine.

"Don't be. I'm not." She looked at him, smiling. "Michael, now that I'm here I feel even better. I missed it here. New York is my home. Just when I was getting used to it, I up and left. I want to finish my degree. I only missed one semester. First thing tomorrow I'm going to make some phone calls. At least I will be around for the holidays!"

"I have to say, I'm really glad you are back. And you're lucky, the Bartoloni's didn't rent that apartment yet."

"Good, looks like I need a place to stay before heading back to school." Luisa was happy she would be able to stay in the same building.

****

Luisa never called Mitchell to tell him she was coming back. He thought she was making a big mistake heading to Paris and pushing school off.

"No offense but didn't you push school off long enough as it is?" he had told her when she gave him the news.

"I'm not going to take offense to your crack at my age. It's never too late to go back," she said before she left for Paris.

"Well, I might be outta here before you return which, let's be honest, you're probably not returning." He was sad.

"Mitchell I am. I will be back. This is temporary."

"Yeah ok." He didn't believe her.

She knew where he and his friends ate dinner and her first night headed over there.

"Bonjour!" she said out loud.

They all turned and Mitchell got up. His initial reaction was to hug her. "You're back? Already?" After realizing the awkward almost hug he stopped. "So, what happened?"

"I will tell you after you give me that hug!" She then hugged him. She heard his friends giggle like girls and Mitchell turned bright red.

99

"Well, turns out Paris wasn't for me. I also figured you boys needed me. Who else will make sure you do your laundry and eat well!"

"It's good to see you, Luisa," one of them said.

"It's certainly nice being back."

The rest of the semester went quick. She even managed to spend her spring break back on the vineyard. When she returned to school, Luisa really concentrated on her studies and thought about taking summer courses but remembered that she told Giuseppe she would be back for the summer.

She called him the next morning to see how he was. Things were not good for him and she could hear it in his voice. She knew what it was she must do.

She explained to Michael that she had to go back to California and be there for her children. The time was coming. Michael knew how difficult this was for her. They had discussed it many times before. He couldn't imagine witnessing his own children growing old. It was all strange to him. He saw for himself though, Luisa never aged. Since he was a young boy. Not even a little. He remembered one night, while sitting around after first moving to New York, they were bored one evening.

"Show me how fast you heal," he said, as if asking her to order Chinese food.

"What? No, Michael I can't do that. I'm not a freak show!" She looked at him as if he was crazy.

"Oh come on!" He threw a pillow at her.

They laughed about it for a moment more, and then she got a knife and made a very tiny cut in her hand by her thumb. "Never try this on yourself you understand?"

"No shit! What am I stupid?"

She shook her head laughing.

He would always remember how strange it was to see her heal instantly. She took a tissue and wiped away the blood as if it was a stain on her skin.

Michael knew that Luisa missed her children. He knew that no matter how old they got, deep down they were still her children and she knew and felt she had to watch over them and protect them.

She always told them how crazy it was that we all start off so helpless, relying on our mothers. Now, as they got older and just as helpless, as their mother, she was going to be there for them again.

Two days after classes ended, she was scheduled to head back to California. She did not tell anyone she was arriving. It was her house after all. She could come and go as she pleased. They even left her bedroom vacant in case she ever wanted to come back.

Michael dropped her off at the airport. "I feel like we are always here lately."

"Seems that way doesn't it?" she laughed.

They looked at each other seriously. Luisa took his hands in hers, "Listen, as soon as I'm not needed I'm coming back to take care of you, ok?"

"Do I look like I need to be taken care of?"

"No, but I want to."

They hugged each other and he wished her a safe trip.

When she got off the plane the nostalgia was all around her. It was in the air. She couldn't wait to get to the vineyard. She rented a car so she could enjoy the ride alone and think about all that she had accomplished so far.

She started from the beginning as she entered the green and brown hills. Starting off as a little girl, growing up on a vineyard, falling in love for the first time with Giovanni, her life with Lorenzo and raising three wonderful children, experiencing San Francisco, moving to New York, getting a degree in teaching and now she can say she even lived in Paris for a bit. A very short bit but still was able to say it. Who else can say they did all of that and still looked at good as she did.

She started to think about the real reason she was heading back home. Her emotions started to get the best of her.

How can it be? How can you witness your baby growing into an old man? She thought of all the children. Mario and Maria as well. She remembered them kicking the ball around with Giovanni those days he and his family came to visit their home in Sicily. She remembered when they climbed up on Lorenzo's back as tired as he was from a hard day of working and yet he couldn't help but laugh with them. He really loved them all. She wished things had gone differently. She really would have loved to grow old with him. Openly be his partner as they watched their children and grandchildren grow. So many times she would apologize to him and he would immediately stop her. They each blamed themselves for what happened. He said he was grateful that she would be around to take care of the family. And now she was going to do just that. She would be there for them for as long as they needed her. After all, she seemed to have all the time in the world.

She pulled up to the vineyard. Nobody was out front so she walked around to the back door, which opened up into the kitchen area.

Her granddaughter saw her first, well her great-granddaughter. There was a point she didn't bother with using 'great' anymore. She just called them all her grandchildren.

"Luisa!" the little girl yelled, and ran over to her.

Luisa laughed loud throwing her arms around her. "Oh I missed it here so much!"

She looked up and saw Giuseppe walking with a cane. He really did move slower. Since the wedding he seemed to age so much more. He looked weaker than last time.

When he saw her his face said how he truly felt with her being there. He put his arms out for her to come to him and they embraced each other for a moment.

Giuseppe led her into the living room where Mario had been sitting watching his grandchildren play.

"Mario, look who is here," Giuseppe said to him.

The tears immediately flowed in his eyes at the sight of his mother. Seeing her always brought back memories of his childhood. He couldn't believe she still looked the same way she did all those years ago. Even though it was only a few years since he last saw her, deep down he worried he wouldn't see her again. Mario got up as Luisa ran over to him.

"Oh my baby. I'm here now. I want to spend time with you all again. It's where I belong."

He looked her in the eyes and all he could say was, "Remarkable."

That night Maria came by for dinner. It was great to see all of the newer generation in the kitchen, cooking and cleaning. Luisa was not allowed to help out, she was to sit and enjoy her time with Giuseppe, Mario and Maria along with Mario's wife and Maria's husband. Sadly, Giuseppe's wife passed away a few years earlier.

They sat and laughed about their life growing up and the troubles they got into with Lorenzo who was very stern at times. Luisa told them all about New York and how fast paced it was compared to living on the vineyard and in the mountains. Maria updated her on all their friends, the family members who passed and the ones who were expecting babies.

As the weeks went by, Luisa noticed that Giuseppe was getting weaker and weaker. They all smoked and you could hear it in his lungs when he coughed. She took him to his doctor visits, which were ever more frequent, even though Giuseppe insisted that he was fine and didn't need to go back. One morning she had to fight to get him to go.

"Giuseppe! You need to go to your appointment now, stop being difficult!"

"Doctors, they just kill you. If the time comes where you have to go to the doctor's office every day then that's it, you might as well say goodnight. Then again, I'm tired. I had enough already."

Giuseppe started coughing and for a moment lost his breath.

"Now you stop that nonsense talking you hear me!" Luisa put his jacket on and managed to get him walking to the car.

It started to get difficult and stressful for Luisa as time went on. Giuseppe was not being himself. He would get angry at every little thing.

One night his daughter-in-law placed his plate in front of him at the table loaded with food. He looked at it with a nasty look, took a bite and pushed the plate across the table. "How do you expect me to eat this? It's cold! What's the matter with you?"

They were all used to it and Luisa told them all she would take care of it. She remembered how Lorenzo got towards the end as well and it was bringing back all those memories. She heated the food up for him again, and even though he still was not completely satisfied with it he ate it, complaining the entire time there was no flavor.

Luisa was awoken one night from Giuseppe's coughing. They decided to take him to the emergency room where they kept him overnight.

After three hours of waiting, Luisa, along with Giuseppe's son Frank, were approached by the doctor.

"His lungs are not looking so good. All that smoking has caught up to him and he's having a very difficult time breathing. For now, we have him on oxygen and will continue to monitor him. I can't say how well he will do and I'm not sure if he will be able to return home."

Frank asked, "Is he dying? I mean, could it happen soon?"

"It's hard to tell. It's all really up to him." At that, the doctor patted Frank's shoulder and stepped away.

Luisa looked at Frank who seemed to be holding tears back. "It's ok to cry, my love." Frank hugged Luisa and cried in her arms.

It was about 6:00 in the morning when Luisa told Frank to go home and rest up. She said that she would watch over Giuseppe. She headed back into his room and sat next to him holding his hand the entire time. It was moments like this that Luisa did not think she would be able to handle.

103

Giuseppe passed away with most of the family surrounding him. Many friends showed up for his funeral and wake, it was a lovely ceremony. Even Michael and Katherine came.

"So how long are you planning on staying in California?" Michael asked Luisa while handing her a glass of wine.

"Well, I'd like to be here for Mario and Maria as long as they need me to." Luisa was so upset over Giuseppe's passing and the thought of watching two other children die was too much for her.

"You know, Luisa…you took care of everyone for so long. You don't have to feel guilty for not being there in case anything happens. It's really a lot for someone to handle. Most people do not have to deal with what you are. These are your children. I mean, yes over the years it might not seem that way anymore but if it's too much emotionally…I just don't think you need to deal with such sadness."

"He's right Luisa." They both turned to see Maria holding on to Mario's arm. "You know we love you but we will be fine. Go back and finish school. Why do you want to hang around with us old folks?"

Mario laughed, "Speak for yourself. I still have a good 15 years ahead of me!" They all laughed.

Maria walked over and put her hands up on Michael's shoulders. "Luisa, we need you to take care of this boy here. We can take care of ourselves."

Luisa stayed for another week and headed back to New York. She managed to sign up last minute for some classes and bought a condo close to school along with a car. It was time she started living on her own like a grown-up should.

Chapter 18

About a year after the wedding, Michael gave Luisa a phone call asking if they could come pay her a visit that coming weekend. Of course she was delighted at this. Michael and Katherine were the closest family to her and she loved every minute she got to spend with them. She had a lot of schoolwork lately so she wasn't able to take trips often to see them, so the fact that they would come to her made her ecstatic. Luisa decided to make a big meal for them. Katherine had asked if she could show her how to make certain meals and Luisa wrote everything down for her and told her if they came early enough she could even show her a couple of the recipes.

That Saturday they arrived around 1:00 pm. Luisa already had food in the oven and sauce cooking on the stove. Her apartment wasn't the biggest but she purposely got a two bedroom for the times when Michael did wish to visit.

Luisa had bought some crackers and cheese to put out on the table along with some mixed nuts. She offered iced tea, agreeing to save the wine for dinner. They sat around her kitchen table for half an hour talking about how married life was and how Luisa's teachers were. She was not especially fond of her English teacher, who she felt was rude to her and made her feel as if she was foolish for returning to school at an older age. After much complaining and talking on Luisa's part, Michael decided it was time to cut in.

"So, you know, we came here for a reason. There was something we wanted to let you know." Michael had his arms crossed on the table and was leaning inward, facing Luisa with a smirk on his face.

Luisa didn't say a word. She looked at Michael then at Katherine and asked, "What are you going to tell me?"

"Well." Michael looked over at Katherine and smiled. "We are going to have a baby!"

Luisa screamed so loud that it made them both laugh and Michael covered his ears. "Jeeze Luise!" he said.

"Oh I can't wait! It's been so long since I have held a baby!"

Katherine laughed, "Well I have to say being pregnant is not all that fun! I need to use the bathroom again, I'll be right back." She got up and headed down the hall.

The rest of the visit was wonderful and Luisa couldn't have been happier for them.

With awaiting the arrival of Michael and Katherine's baby, Luisa tried her best to be more involved with everything. She was always in contact with Katherine's family for the planning of the baby shower and helping them pick out whatever it was they needed.

The months flew by and one evening Luisa's phone rang in the middle of the night. It was Michael. He called to tell her that he was taking Katherine to the hospital; it was time. Being that it was summertime and Luisa did not take any classes this semester she got in her car and drove to the hospital to be there with them. It was a long night, Luisa had fallen asleep along with Katherine's family in the waiting room. They were all awoken by Michael coming through the doors yelling, "It's a boy! I have a baby boy!"

They all got up and hugged him asking who the baby looked like. Michael couldn't answer and said, "Like all babies look like, he's too young to look like us."

Luisa gave Michael the longest hug. "Listen, I'll go back to your apartment and cook you some food so that you guys have it all week ok?"

"Only if you promise to sleep first, you look like hell." Michael said to her, jokingly.

"Yeah well all I ate in the last 10 hours were candy bars and soda from the machines!"

Michael had insisted that Luisa keep her key from the apartment after she moved out so she was able to just go ahead and settle in. As soon as she arrived she decided she would sleep a bit and then head out to the store to buy some food to cook all day.

She wasn't even up the walkway and Mr. and Mrs. Bartoloni were at the front door. Mrs. Bartoloni was so excited to see Luisa. "Luisa! How is everything? Good? What is it? Boy o girl?"

"A beautiful boy! Mommy and daddy are doing just fine too." Luisa said with a smile. "I'm going to go inside and take a nap, it's been a long night." She headed down the stairs.

A few hours later Luisa headed out to the supermarket and purchased a ton of food to fill the kitchen with for when they returned. After cooking and freezing some meals she went back to the hospital with a change of clothes for Michael. She was surprised he didn't come back yet to shower and get some sleep himself.

She asked the front desk which room Katherine was staying in and headed in that direction. As she almost entered the room a doctor was just leaving and she smiled and greeted him. All he did was nod his head and continue to walk out of the room.

Katherine was sitting up in the bed and Michael was sitting on the edge hugging her. At first Luisa assumed it was a moment they were having, happy upon the arrival of their new baby but she noticed that Katherine was crying. And certainly not a happy cry.

"What is it? What's going on? Is the baby ok?" Luisa was worried now.

Michael stood up and looked at Luisa, he too had been crying. Luisa's stomach dropped.

He started to shake his head as if he couldn't understand. "We don't know. The doctor just told us that his lungs aren't developed enough. He might not be strong enough on his own. They are watching him now but they don't know Luisa. Oh my God, why my baby? Why?" He started to cry and cover his face with his hands. Luisa rushed over to him holding him tight.

"Ok, come on now. Let's not worry, things will be fine. Let's just think positive, ok?" She then moved to the bed to hold Katherine's hand as well. "Everything is going to be good, ok? Now come on, let's start praying."

About half an hour later Katherine's parents came, Luisa left to give them time alone with Michael and Katherine.

"I'm going to go see if I can talk to the doctor." And Luisa headed out of the room. She found the doctor talking to a nurse at the front desk.

She walked over to him. "Excuse me, can you please explain to me what is going on with the baby? The Messina baby?"

The doctor did his best to explain it in further detail. There was nothing they could do but wait and see how he did. That evening Michael's parents were flying in from California. Luisa picked them up from the airport and took them right to the hospital. Even though visiting hours were over, the nurse let them in to see Michael and Katherine. Luisa waited in the lobby for them.

As they were asked to leave, Michael's father insisted that he come down to the lobby to have a talk with them and Luisa. Michael told Katherine he would be right back. They headed down the elevator and met Luisa in the lobby. They asked Luisa to join them in a more quiet area where there were less people.

Michael's father, Frank, sat next to Luisa and everyone sat facing each other. He looked at Luisa and took her hand in his. "Luisa, we know that you are the only one who could help us here."

Luisa looked puzzled. "Me? Whatever could I do? I would do whatever it takes, you know that Frank."

He looked at his wife who nodded as if telling him to proceed. "You see, there is something special about you. Perhaps if you were able to give the baby the gift that was given to you, maybe the baby will have a better chance."

"Frank, how on earth could I do that when I don't even know myself what is wrong with me! I don't know how this happened to me! If I knew myself don't you think I would be using this power all the time? What is it that I can do?"

Michael looked just as puzzled but thought more about it after hearing it coming from his father. "Well, maybe it's in your blood. I mean has anyone even tried to use your blood for anything? What if the baby received some of your blood?"

Luisa got upset from hearing this. How on earth did they think that any doctor would allow such a thing. Not to mention this was the one thing that they were to avoid. Any doctors going near Luisa. Of course she wanted to help the baby, after all he was her family as well. But they were all asking the impossible and not thinking straight. Her blood was not going to cure his lungs. Even she knew this, how could they possibly think it could. She was surprised that Michael even considered this but she also understood that right now Michael was probably desperate to hear any solution.

"This is crazy and you all know it. You don't just take blood from someone and administer it into another person! That's not how things work." She still couldn't believe what she was hearing, but started to feel horrible when she saw the look on everyone's face.

Frank seemed to get upset now. "It certainly doesn't hurt to ask!"

"Ask? Ask what? The doctor? Would you like to walk up to the doctor and tell him that I am really from the late 1800's and have been living ever since? Perhaps if he takes my blood and gives it right to the baby then the baby will be fine and live forever! Well let's just say now that we do this and for some odd reason the doctor does this, which we all know is not going to happen because the doctor will kick us out of the hospital or maybe send us all to the psych ward, let's just say we did this. Do you now understand what it is that I am going through? I have not aged. Do you want your baby to stay two days old forever? What happens when you grow old and die? Would you want to have the same baby that is too young to see you fully and too young to laugh? Do you want a baby that never grows up and plays and laughs loud? Think about it. Think about how absolutely insane this all sounds!" She looked over at Michael. "Think of what Katherine would think. She would go out of her mind not understanding any of this."

Nobody said a word until finally Michael stood up. "Luisa is right. This would never work and even if it did, it's not the life we want for our baby." He looked over at Luisa. "I'm sorry."

"Michael, do not be sorry! You are going through a hard time and you have to know that I would do anything for that baby. Please, know that."

He walked over and hugged her. "Of course I do. I know. I'm going to go back to Katherine."

Frank and his wife did not seem as understanding and made Luisa feel she was being selfish. She realized that they were simply uneducated and it was impossible to explain anything to them.

"We should head home." Luisa started to walk toward the exit. Frank and his wife got up and followed.

The next few weeks were difficult but each day the baby showed improvement and it turned out that he was going to be just fine. The day came to take the baby home and Luisa greeted them at the door. Katherine's parents drove them all back to the apartment. That night they all celebrated at the Bartoloni's apartment. Luisa was going to head home first thing the next day. Katherine headed downstairs early to feed the baby and put him to sleep.

They named him Joseph in honor of Giuseppe only decided the American version of his name would be more appropriate.

Michael and Luisa walked Katherine's parents out to the car to get some fresh air themselves. After they pulled away Luisa looked over at Michael. "Michael, I feel really bad about that night with your parents in the lobby of the hospital. You know I would have done anything for Joseph."

"Luisa! Stop!" He took her by the shoulders. "Forget about that night. My parents are stupid, they don't understand anything. I said what I did because I was desperate. It was crazy to even think any doctor would even listen to us. Come on, let's go inside."

The next morning on the drive home, Luisa did a lot of thinking. She never thought about the possibility of being able to help others. If she did look into this it could mean trouble for her. Lorenzo always stressed how this must be kept a secret, nobody could ever find out about her. But what if it was possible? She was relieved that the baby turned out fine and there was no need for her to feel guilty for not trying. She also knew that it wouldn't have been in her control anyway, no doctor would have believed them. All she could do is continue to live the way she has and not let anyone else know her secret. As hard as it may be.

Chapter 19

2018

"Excuse me, Ms. Medina? When you get a minute, can you come to my office? "

"Of course, I will be done here in 15 minutes." Luisa smiled graciously at Sue Higgins. A ton of questions raced through her head. Like what could she possibly have to ask me? Sue ran the records department at the High School where Luisa was teaching. Luisa hoped there wasn't a problem. She wondered if it had anything to do with records not matching up.

Many years ago, Michael, had set her up on two different occasions with new sets of identification. He had a close friend who once worked in the government and had connections with people who were able to provide Luisa with fake identification whenever she needed it. She had to change her social security number, her name, and her entire identity. Always though, she requested her first name be kept and last name similar for the sake of less confusion. The first time was when she moved to New York. Her son Giuseppe somehow managed a new social security number. All he did was take out one letter in her last name to keep it similar. She never asked him how he did it. Back then, her son knew many people and everyone helped everyone out when needed. No questions asked. She went from Messina to Mesina. Then, Mesina to Mesinna, Mesinna to Medina. She figured at this rate one day she could go back to her original name. Her latest change was only a little over five years ago. She noticed over time it was more difficult to get away with these kinds of things. National Security was on top of everything. Thankfully, Michael's friend, who was now retired, entrusted Michael and knew this was not something to be concerned about. He didn't want to know. Not that he would have believed it anyway.

It was hard to believe that Michael was now in his late 60's. Just like her son Giuseppe, Michael became very protective of Luisa. She was so grateful for him in her life. Giuseppe, Maria and Mario's deaths were hard on her. Thankfully, their deaths were all due to old age but it was still very frustrating. Over time, she learned to deal with the situation that was handed to her. The only person she let get close to her was Michael. Men came and went but she ended it when it became

111

serious. She knew she could never love again. Besides, nobody lived up to Lorenzo. To be even more honest, nobody ever lived up to Giovanni. Even though it was so long ago, she never forgot the way she felt for him. She loved Lorenzo, but she had been *in love* with Giovanni.

Luisa grabbed her belongings and started to head down to Sue's office. Over the years, Luisa ended up getting her degree in teaching and after graduation, worked at schools in Queens, NY. She wanted to be close enough to Michael who lived in the suburbs of the city with his family. After about fifteen years, she knew it was time to move on. People always complemented her on her youthful looks, but how much longer could she push it? Michael got her the new identity and she took a job teaching at a school out by him. Michael had the new birth certificate say that she was in her late 20's so that Luisa could ride it out a little longer. People might talk about how young you look for your age but they would never dare say you looked older. She could deal with knowing what they might be thinking. She really could get away with being ten years younger anyway. She also changed her first name to Louise. A more American name seemed appropriate. Michael even managed to have references from out of state at schools that she apparently worked for.

Luisa knocked on Sue's door before entering.

"Come in! Oh, hi Louise. Thanks for coming down. I won't be long at all." She motioned to an available seat in front of her desk.

"No problem, I'm finished up for today anyway. So, what's up?" Luisa was prepared to answer any issues that might have arisen with her paperwork. She's now been around long enough to deal with every situation and keep her initial reactions masked.

"Well, I just thought I would let you know something. A man called this morning asking some questions about you. When I asked where he was from, he said he was just confirming employment. Now, Louise, it's none of my business if you are looking to work elsewhere. It's just he started to ask me questions that I didn't find relevant to verifying employment." Sue looked down with confusion on her face. "He asked me if I was aware if you once resided in Sicily. Now, I told him that I could not provide him with such information. He was apologetic and I must say spoke very eloquently."

At hearing this, Luisa's stomach turned a bit but she managed to show no reaction. Instead, she smiled and chuckled. "Well, my parents are from there but I was raised here in America." She couldn't figure out why someone would ask that let alone why anyone was even calling to confirm her employment. There was no family she kept in touch with back in Sicily. Even if there was, they would never think to contact her since she would have passed away so long ago. "Also, I am definitely not looking for work elsewhere. Thank you for your concern though. If that's all Sue I'd better be heading out now." Luisa got up and headed toward the door.

Sue gave a little laugh herself. "Yes, well perhaps he was just inquiring. He said he himself was from a town called Salemi I believe. Yes, that's it, I wrote it down. Habit I suppose. I always take notes."

At hearing that, Luisa stopped and held the doorknob so tight. She had never met anyone who claimed to be from Salemi besides her own family. She had to take a few deep breaths before she could speak again.

"Louise? Is everything ok?" Sue asked as she stood up, noticing Luisa standing there staring at the door.

"Excuse me? Oh, yes. Sorry Sue. I was just trying to remember where I left something. Thanks again." As she opened the door and headed out, she stopped and turned to Sue once more. "Listen, do you think I could get the number of the person who called? It usually comes up on the phone right?"

"Actually it came up unknown. I was curious myself." Sue seemed disappointed.

"Right, ok no worries." Luisa left and walked towards the exit.

On her way to the car, Luisa made a phone call to Michael.

"Hi, it's me. Listen, something strange happened today. I was told by the office that a man was asking about me."

Michael laughed, "Well it's about time. Maybe you can keep this one!"

"No! Not like that. Someone called the office. They asked if I was from Sicily and apparently, they grew up in Salemi. Michael that is where I grew up. How can someone know that? I mean, it has been over 100 years!"

"Maybe it was just someone looking into their heritage. Lately that seems like the thing to do. I'm sure there is no connection at all and just a coincidence. Are you coming by Saturday? Hello? Are you there?"

"What?" Luisa was distracted.

"Saturday, Joseph's graduation! You're... let's see now. That would make him your great-great-grandson? Ha ha!" Michael found this amusing.

"Oh yes. I'll be there." Luisa wasn't in a joking mood.

When she got home, she quickly opened up a bottle of red wine. Poured a glass and opened the fridge looking for something to heat up for dinner. Luisa tried to cook large portions on the weekends to eat during the week. Cooking for one person was more of a hassle. Sometimes she even caved in and bought a frozen meal. She would laugh at the thought of ever serving one of those to Lorenzo when they were married. Things were so convenient. She would keep a small pan of food in her new oven/refrigerator. You kept it cold during the day and set a timer, which started to heat up like an oven. By the time you got home dinner was ready. Not only that, this could be controlled through your phone from wherever you were. She couldn't understand why these things had not been invented earlier. It really made life easy.

Forgetting to put something in the oven this morning, she grabbed a container of chicken and rice and placed it in the microwave while she changed. On her way to the bedroom, she said out loud "Screen on. Messages first, then TV. Channel 30." It was amazing how far technology had come since her days on the farm.

An electronic voice sensed which room she entered and would speak in that room.

"Good Evening Luisa. Message one…"

She listened to a message from Michael. "Yeah. Luisa. Saturday they are having a graduation dinner for Joseph. It's last minute, you know these kids. They'd rather hang out with their friends instead but his mother told him he would probably make some money from the family so that changed his mind quickly. Anyway, come by around 5 o'clock. Ok. See you then."

The electronic voice spoke again, "Next message…"

It was a man's voice this time that she did not recognize. "Hi, I was hoping to speak to a Louise Medina. My name is John Tola. I uh, well I just had a couple of questions I would like to ask you. I'm not even sure if I have the right person. I'm doing some research on a book I'm writing. It's regarding vineyards in Sicily. I was just hoping maybe we could chat about your childhood living on a vineyard. That is, if I have the right person. If you are interested, please give me a call. My number is 555-498-2110. My video number is the same with a five at the end. 555-498-2115. I hope to hear from you Louise."

She sat on the edge of her bed confused.

"Final message…"

"Luisa? Ok, it's me again. Yeah, bring some of that cheese cake you made last time."

The television turned on to the cooking channel. Brandon Hall was on. He was the latest and greatest. He was making eggplant parmesan. He called it Old World Cuisine. Luisa was about to say something to the computer until she looked at the screen and laughed.

"Really? Everyone knows you have to salt the eggplant first! UGH. Computer search. John Tola."

Brandon's face was quickly replaced with a search engine on the screen. The electronic voice was back. "John Tola. Author of *Beauty in Europe,* which consists of drawings from all over Europe."

"Stop. Images." Luisa needed to know why this person assumed she grew up in Sicily, on a vineyard nonetheless.

Images started to appear on the screen. Luisa's hands went cold and her glass of red wine dropped to the floor all over her white carpet.

Chapter 20

"Who's knocking at this time?" Michael seemed annoyed and wondered why his wife wasn't getting the front door. "Where the hell is everyone? Oh for crying out loud!" He got up and went to the door. It was Luisa. She had a panicked look on her face. "Shouldn't you be home making a cheesecake?"

"Michael. Michael, I don't know what's happening! It can't be. I mean it can't! Can it? That man, the man who called earlier? He left a message for me. He wanted to interview me for a book he's writing on vineyards in Sicily or something like that." She walked in and looked at him for a response.

Michael looked at her, sat back down, and looked at the TV. "Luisa. It's impossible for anyone to know anything! He probably got your name confused with someone who actually *did* live there! Recently! It's that simple! You are going crazy in your old age I tell you."

Luisa looked annoyed. She sat next to him. "TV OFF!"

The screen went blank. Michael looked at her. "Oh come on! Do you really think someone said let me interview this woman who is, oh, 150 years old? Come on Luisa! Think! I'm too old for this!"

She looked him in the eyes. "Michael. There is something you don't know. You remember when your grandfather told you the story about me?"

"Yes. Something about a fire and an old lady." He seemed more annoyed than anything.

She proceeded to tell him the entire story, all about Giovanni and how he was also in the fire but died. She told him how the entire family left shortly after. "They told me he died Michael. Well, I know this sounds crazy but, the man who called me, he looks an awful lot like Giovanni. I mean, if I was saved maybe he was too! And his name! He called himself John! Just like I switched my name to the English version! He could have as well!" She was hysterical; fearful was more like it. If this was Giovanni everything would change. She knew this was a possibility. Her hands literally shook.

Michael sat up on the edge of the couch. "Why didn't you tell me all of this earlier?"

116

"I didn't want you to think badly of me Michael. I did nothing wrong. I loved Lorenzo so much. But my heart always belonged to Giovanni." She started to cry.

"I would never think badly of you! I thought it was crazy they made everyone get married so young back then. On top of it, you had to marry who you were told to. Of course I would understand!" He took Luisa's hand. "Oh Luisa, don't cry. We will call this man." He looked in her eyes to get her full attention. "You understand this might not be him. It could all be a coincidence. I don't want you to get upset again, Luisa."

"It's him Michael!" She laughed through the tears. "I know it is!"

After a little over an hour, Luisa headed home. Michael was able to calm her down and they decided that first thing tomorrow they would call John together. It was a long night, full of emotion and Luisa was exhausted. She still had some work to go over before heading to bed but she knew it would be near impossible to concentrate on it. Perhaps she would call in sick tomorrow. How could she even concentrate on work anyway? Calling in sick meant calling John earlier, which sounded like the best option for her fraying nerves.

Luisa pulled up into the driveway, put the car in park and just sat there for a moment remembering her days with Giovanni. She had done this so frequently for fear of losing the memory. It was so ridiculously long ago.

1886

I quickly cleaned up after dinner with all the other women.

"Why are you in such a hurry tonight?" my mother asked in a suspicious voice.

"Anna wants me to go with her for a walk." I didn't even look up at her and continued to dry a plate. "She had a small fight with her sister and doesn't want to be around her tonight."

"Ok, just make sure you're home before its dark out," she said.

After finishing I ran over to Anna who was putting some pots away. "Hi, do you think you can do me a huge favor tonight?"

117

Anna looked at me knowing what it had to do with and rolled her eyes. "Luisa! Again? You are going to see Giovanni aren't you?"

Looking very guilty, I managed to give her a smile.

"And what am I supposed to do? Now I have to hide out somewhere!" Anna was not thrilled with this.

"I will make it up to you I promise! Whatever you want! Please Anna!" I now started to beg for fear of the thought of not being able to meet with Giovanni.

"FINE!" Anna scowled.

Throwing my arms around her, I gave her a kiss on the cheek. "Ok meet me out back in ten minutes so we can walk off together!"

About fifteen minutes later Anna waited outside. "You're late!"

I saw that she was holding a book and assumed she would be spending her time alone reading. Anna had covered for me on a few different occasions. I knew the second Anna needed me to cover for her I would in an instant. Anna was my closest friend. We could talk about anything. I shifted my hip in a flirty fashion, "You know, I noticed that Tanino had been looking at you the other day. Perhaps that favor would come up soon enough, eh?"

Anna hit me with the book. We both headed off down the hill as my mother yelled from behind, "Remember to be back before it's dark out girls!"

We stopped near a large tree that was not visible to the vineyard. Anna sat down and opened her book, "Remember, not too long Luisa!"

Looking back at her with a big grin, I ran off to where Giovanni planned to meet me. There was a creek not too far from there surrounded by many trees. I arrived but there was no sight of Giovanni. I went down to where there was a big rock by the water and I sat on it waiting. It wasn't long before I heard Giovanni whistling.

"Would you like some company young lady!" As I turned, Giovanni had a silly look on his face.

We spent the next hour enjoying each other's company, talking about how our lives would be when we were older, and how our children would look. Noticing the sun setting, we decided to head back.

That night, I went to bed dreaming about my future and praying to God that Giovanni would be part of it.

****

Exhausted emotionally from the thought of seeing Giovanni after so many years, Luisa got slowly out of her car and headed down the walkway. She knew she would need to get a solid night's sleep if she were to call this person tomorrow with Michael. It could all just be a coincidence and the resemblance could be something she created in her head. She wasn't sure why though. She never did this before with anyone else.

Heading up the stairs to the front door, she heard a car door open from behind her. Turning around to look, she saw a man approaching her. His mouth was covered by his hands as he looked as astonished as she did.

He removed his hands from his face and put one hand out towards her, "Luisa, oh my God. It really is you."

She slowly started to walk towards him, tears in her eyes. She could hardly make out his name, "Giovanni!"

They just stood there looking at each other. He then grabbed her face in his hands and just stared at her, as if touching her would make this real. Shaking his head in disbelief, he grabbed her so close to him she could hardly breathe.

"How can this be?" she sobbed.

After holding each other for a few minutes, they sat on the front steps to her house. She didn't think she could physically make it inside. The shock was too much.

Giovanni was sobbing himself. Still shaking his head he said, "They told me you didn't make it. I felt in my heart though, I felt you were still alive!"

"It's been so long Giovanni! So long." Her head was on his shoulder. They stood there just holding each other for a while. She looked up at him, "Come inside."

He practically carried her to the door. Her hands shook so much she could hardly open the door with the key.

"Would you like some wine? If not, I know I need some!" She went into the kitchen to get a bottle and two glasses. Giovanni sat down on one of the couches. He was still in shock himself. All he kept thinking was how much time was wasted. He heard the cork pop and the rattle of glasses. He quickly got up to help Luisa but he almost knocked into her on the way towards the kitchen.

"Oh! Sorry!" He wasn't thinking straight. Luisa laughed and motioned back to the couch. She put the two glasses on the coffee table. Giovanni had taken the bottle from her and proceeded to pour them both a glass, a very full glass. They both clicked their glasses together lightly and drank still looking at each other in disbelief.

"So, how did you find me? It sure took you long enough." They both laughed at the comment knowing how long it truly was. More than anyone can imagine.

"After the fire, all I can remember is lying in bed. Even when I woke up and felt better, I didn't want to get up. My brother told me that you didn't make it. I felt so responsible. I felt that if I never approached you in the first place you never would have been in that position, that you would still be alive if I hadn't seen you again. I hated myself for doing that. I hated that because of me your children lost their mother." Giovanni started to get angry. His face was full of rage and he banged his hand on the coffee table "If only they didn't lie to me! Everything could have been better!"

"Giovanni, please don't get upset. I felt the same way when they told me you died in the fire. We can't be angry anymore. It was so long ago."

Giovanni laughed, which confused Luisa. He sat back and smiled at her, "You know, I have not been called Giovanni for a very long time. It sounds so strange to hear you say that name...Louise!" they both laughed.

Luisa was grateful the anger had gone quickly, but she had so many questions still.

"Gio- John, what did your grandmother do to us? For so long I had no idea. What will become of our lives?" She looked at him with desperation hoping he had all the answers she was looking for all of these years.

Giovanni continued, "I managed to accept it all for the children's sake. I had to go on for them. They knew nothing, as did my wife. When the children were old enough I left. I guess you can call me a coward but I wanted nothing to do with that life on the vineyard. I wanted nothing to do with my wife either. It never got better only worse. Even the children turned against me. She managed to do that. My grandmother went to live with other relatives shortly after I was better. I had no idea at the time what was going to happen to me. Yes, I noticed that I was looking good as the years went by, young and healthy still. I didn't think anything of it to be honest. I moved to Palermo and got involved doing work there. I went back home after a few years. My brother told me my wife took the children and moved in with her family. Then he said they received a letter from cousin Franco that grandma had passed away. She left something for me. It was a letter and a necklace. Nothing fancy but it was gold with a charm in the shape of a tree. The letter said that after many years I would be confused with the way things might be turning out. That I shouldn't fear it, but accept it. She said the necklace is a symbol of life. She said trees can live for over a hundred years or more."

Giovanni pulled out the necklace from under his shirt to show Luisa. "I have worn it ever since."

"May I?" She motioned to touch it and he nodded his head in approval.

"I really didn't know what to expect or what was going on. I knew that I had been hurt on many occasions and healed instantly. I never discussed this with anyone. How could I? I felt lost and alone. It was then I decided that I was going to move to America. I knew of a friend that was going and asked if I could tag along. I ended up in New York. Found a job and a place to live in Brooklyn. During my quiet time alone I would draw a lot."

Luisa was thrilled to hear this, "Oh you *did* keep it up! I'm so happy for you Giovanni!"

He laughed a bit, "Yeah, well you were the one who encouraged me to start it up again. Anyway, I drew places I remembered being at in Italy. They looked so good I decided to start painting them. I hung one up in the restaurant I worked at and one of the patrons asked if it was for sale. The owner asked if I had any more paintings and he let me hang them up with prices under them. They all sold. He got a percentage and I made a nice savings for myself. I decided to travel a bit with the extra money. It was time I left there anyway."

Giovanni sat back more comfortably now and took a sip of wine. It made Luisa feel relaxed as well so she also sat back, leaning towards him listening. Right now life could not have gotten better for her. Everything was right, the mood, the wine and Giovanni sitting next to her.

Giovanni continued, "So I traveled all around Europe and painted all the wonderful places I had visited. When I returned to America, I stopped by to see the owner of the restaurant that sold my paintings and he told me there were people asking if I had any more for sale. So, I sold the ones I had done during my travels. Anything to make a buck right?" He looked at her and winked. Luisa could feel the pang in her stomach. She smiled back and drank more wine hoping he didn't notice that she was blushing.

"About two weeks ago I was with a few friends. One of them was telling me about a couple of classes she was taking. They lived on the Island. She mentioned your name and I don't know, it just hit something inside of me. Your name was so similar. I asked what you looked like. I mean, Luisa, over the years I always thought it was possible the same thing might have happened to you too. I searched your name but never came up with anything. I actually came up with Lorenzo's name in California. I was even going to go there but stopped myself. I already felt guilty for what had happened. Lorenzo I'm sure would never forget my face.

"Anyway, she told me what you looked like and that you were Sicilian. I had to see for myself. I came to your school and parked outside. It was then that I saw you, Luisa. I wanted to run up to you but I dare not frighten you, just in case. That's why I tried to set up the interview with you. I knew that if I talked to you or if you saw me I would know. Enough about me; tell me all about what you have been up to."

Luisa proceeded to tell him everything. They talked about other lovers they met over the years. Of course, he had more than she did which didn't thrill her, but they moved on quickly from that subject.

He sat forward on the couch thinking aloud, "If only we knew someone who could figure this out. Do some testing on us without causing any alarms. I don't know about you but I certainly have always liked my privacy. I don't want to mess it up. Although finding you Luisa, for the first time ever, I am thrilled to be cursed with this."

They put their glasses down and held hands. Giovanni pulled her closer to him and leaned back on the couch so she could lie on his chest. "I never want to let you go again."

It had been such a long night. They fell asleep from exhaustion. As morning came, the ringing of the telephone had woken them. Luisa abruptly jumped up and looked around, confused at first from being on the couch, but then smiled as she saw Giovanni lying next to her as he slowly opened his eyes.

She got up and put her finger over her mouth, "Shh, go back to sleep, I will be back," She got up and ran to her bedroom saying aloud after closing the door behind her "Answer."

"Louise? It's Sue. Is everything ok?"

Luisa realized she must have slept through the morning and should have been at her class by now. Thank goodness she didn't say "video answer" or Sue would have seen what a mess she was. Although, perhaps that would have helped her in this instance.

"Sue, yes, everything is fine. My apologies. I was up all night with a stomach issue and to be quite honest I must have finally fallen asleep and slept right through the morning. I'm still not feeling very well I'm sorry to say."

Sue replied she was just happy that Luisa was safe at home and hoped she would feel better. The substitute teacher happened to be in the office that morning to pick something up so Sue would see if she wouldn't mind subbing for the day. After hanging up, Luisa looked in the mirror in horror. She immediately ran into the bathroom to brush her teeth and freshen up. It's been too long to let Giovanni see her this way. Before going back inside, she decided to call Michael. He answered quickly.

"Good morning!" she said, obviously in a great mood.

"Hey, good morning. I know why you're so excited but remember don't get your hopes up. This man-" she cut him off.

"Michael, he's here! It's Giovanni! He was here last night waiting for me!"

"What? Who's there?"

Luisa was getting a little annoyed. Michael's hearing was starting to go and he never understood her when she called him. She didn't want Giovanni to hear her either. She tried not to yell too loud but spoke so he could hear her. At first, Michael was nervous that she could be wrong but she knew it was Giovanni and she assured him not to worry.

"I'll call you later tonight, Michael," she said, and hung up.

When she went inside, she saw that Giovanni... John that is, was not on the couch anymore. She did, however, smell coffee coming from the kitchen and headed that way.

"I can't believe you converted to American coffee. What happened to you?" He walked towards her and gave her a kiss on the lips. They both seemed a bit surprised at how natural it felt. They had never gotten intimate with each other aside from a short kiss back when they were young in the vineyards.

123

He looked deep in her eyes and kissed her again. This time it lasted much longer. For the very first time Luisa felt like she had finally expected to feel with someone. This was a feeling like no other. It felt like she had once and for all found what was missing in her life. As if she made it home and was safe.

Holding hands, they walked into her bedroom and slowly made love for most of the day. After taking a nap or two, they were disturbed by a knocking on the front door. Luisa quickly jumped up.

"I wonder who that could be," looking at the time. "Oh my gosh where did the day go! It's nearly 3 pm!" she said as she put her robe on.

Giovanni laughed, "Oh my dear, I can tell you where the day has gone if you allow me!"

She picked up his shirt from the floor and threw it at him, "Come on now! Get out of bed, you must be starving anyway!"

The knocking did not stop, "One minute!" she yelled out, opened the door and saw Michael standing there.

"I came by to make sure you were ok." He pushed past her and walked inside looking all around.

A little surprised she answered him, "Yes I am fine. In fact, I have never been better!"

"So where is he?" Michael didn't seem happy at all. He was turning into a grumpy old man.

From behind a voice spoke, "Here *he* is. That is, if it was me you were referring to."

Giovanni walked towards Michael and extended his hand, "Pleasure to meet you, my name is John Tola."

Michael shook his hand and Luisa interrupted, "This is Michael, he is…well. Believe it or not he is my great grandson!"

"Just remember who's technically older," Michael added. They all laughed, "I just came by to make sure everything was good. I see you didn't go to work today." He looked her up and down and saw she was wearing only a robe. Luisa closed it even more realizing how it may have looked to Michael. He might have been her great grandson but he acted more like her grandfather.

"Yes, Michael. Giovanni and I had a lot of catching up to do. Come and sit down. I want to tell you everything; just let me change." She headed to the bedroom.

Michael sat down and looked up at Giovanni. "Amazing isn't it? I can't believe there is another person out there with the same situation as Luisa. You know, she told me everything; about the two of you that is."

124

Giovanni sat down on the chair opposite side, "I just want you to know, I feel responsible for everything. I never should have agreed to go to their home with my brothers. I should have left as soon as Luisa and I spoke. We had families and…"

Michael cut him off, "Listen, I don't judge you. Remember, I am not from the time you two grew up in. I understand how it was back then. You had your reasons and you can't take blame for something that happened so long ago. In fact, if you hadn't gone there, I would never even know Luisa. If it weren't for Luisa, my life would not be what it is today. It's everything I dreamed of. I would have been stuck working on some vineyard most of my life doing something I never wanted to do. Thanks to her, we came to New York. This is my life and I wouldn't change a thing. So don't go saying you wish *you* did!"

Luisa came out looking at both of them worried, "Is everything ok?"

"Yes, everything is fine." Giovanni smiled at her.

They spent the next hour telling Michael what Giovanni knew. They were sitting around the dining room table eating a meal that Luisa had quickly cooked up. Having Giovanni there brought back some food cravings for pasta and nice homemade sauce. Luckily, she made a pot of sauce and froze it not too long ago. It was as if time went back to the early 1900's being there with Giovanni. Only it was even better because they were able to be free with each other. There was no more hiding from parents or spouses. Not even from children, other workers or relatives. They could actually have a life together out in the open. Finally, what Luisa had been waiting for all this time.

After a long night Michael headed home, "Don't forget to stop by tomorrow. I know you're now busy and everything but you know everyone expects you there." He put his hat on and walked towards the door but stopped and turned around, "Bring John with you."

Chapter 21

The following weeks were all about Luisa and Giovanni spending time together. They promised each other they would never be separated again.

Giovanni lived in the city. He owned a beautiful brownstone in Manhattan, on the Upper East Side. He and Luisa agreed they would go there one Sunday. He wanted to show her all of his drawings and paintings.

The apartment was very rich looking, decorated in a masculine way with dark colors of navy blue and mahogany. There were paintings of all sizes hung everywhere. He led her into a room with only a large, brown leather bench in the center of the room. Each wall was covered with paintings in large gold frames. They all looked like pieces you would see in an art gallery, a museum even by artists long gone. Then again, she realized that Giovanni *had* been around just as long as some of the most famous artists known. Most of the paintings were of well-known historic spots all over the world. Each painting had the same style to it, the same kind of intense focus.

"Giovanni, these are absolutely amazing!"

"If you look, I have these sorted by origin. Over here, this is Spain." He took Luisa's hand and led her closer to one of the paintings. "This one right here, this is the Segovia Castle. It started off as an Arab fort but during the Middle Ages it become home to many kings and queens. Now it's a museum. Hopefully we will visit it together one day, it's truly spectacular." He leaned down and gave her a kiss, then led her to another painting further away. "This one I did after watching a bull fight. I was trying to feel the anger of the animal, show it in his eyes." The painting was a bull in action and showed only his side torso and head. You could see the detail of his face, the passion in his eyes.

"I can see it." Luisa said as she continued to look at the painting.

"Come over here, I want to show you Paris." They walked across the room. She saw right away the painting of The Eiffel Tower. It was drawn as if during the evening, all lit up surrounded by the bridge and Seine River. In the river a large boat was just about to cross under the bridge. That too was lit up. The painting was so life like and solid, as if you could reach out and touch the metal, yet had a softness to it. She could just imagine herself there at the moment. It was too familiar, and as she stared at she thought it had to be the same painting she saw while she was in Paris with Samuel. If it was, she wasn't going to bring that up now. It just made her realize how close she had been to Giovanni at one point even in spirit. If only she had been there when he dropped it off. It's funny, she knew then that there was something about that painting that she connected with, she just didn't know what. Now it was perfectly clear.

She got closer to the painting to see the inscription on the bottom.

"Giovanni Alto." Luisa read it and looked over at Giovanni smiling. "I knew you would make it. So tell me, is this how you got to afford this very expensive townhome in Manhattan?"

Giovanni laughed a little looking down almost ashamed at something.

"What is it?" Luisa asked, smiling herself.

"Well, if you knew all about art you might have heard of me, somehow I became pretty famous in that department. Of course once that happened over time, I never showed my face. I worked directly through an agent and he knew how discrete I wanted to be. I knew then about my situation and wasn't sure how I could get away with it. So I laid low, continuing to paint as many pictures as I could. I did well for myself then but it wasn't until later in life that I was able to profit even more. Let's just say I planned my own death. The late Giovanni Alto had passed away due to a heart attack and his family had him cremated. So, you know what happens when an artist dies right?"

"His paintings are worth more?" Luisa asked.

"Yes, sometimes a lot more. I mean I wasn't as famous as certain painters but let's say my name was out there. People knew me and they liked my stuff. Some even collected my works, so the second they found out I died my paintings were worth a lot more. So what do I do?" He looked at Luisa for the answer.

She looked at him suspiciously. "Sell your own paintings?"

He laughed, "Yes! That is exactly what I did. Nobody knew who I was and most of them are silent auctions. After I faked my own death I changed my name to John Tola. It was easy to do that stuff under the table, you know what I mean."

Luisa shook her head in agreement. "Oh sure. Well, Michael knew the right people to help with that. I didn't really get involved. I would think it would be hard to do now though."

"I agree with you." Giovanni took a deep breath. "Ok, now I want to show you something." He put his hand on her back and pointed down the hall. "After you?"

127

They went into his bedroom. There he had more paintings all over the walls. Large ones and small ones placed here and there in no certain pattern or direction.

"I keep these closer to me so I can see them every day. This my dear, is Sicily."

Luisa walked over to each and every painting. She noticed her homeland right away and felt a pain of longing inside of her. Memories of her childhood, her parents, her friends and of course her family with Lorenzo when they were young, flooded her.

"Luisa?" Giovanni called her over to the other side of the room. There on the wall was a large painting of the vineyard where they met. "If you look close enough, I managed to paint two figures in the vineyard, right here. That is supposed to be you and I the first time we met." He then looked over to see her reaction.

Luisa put her hand to her mouth. It was amazing that all this time he had this and still thought of her.

"I never forgot you Luisa." It was as if he read her mind.

She then hugged him and started to cry. "I just can't believe how long ago all of that was. Sometimes I think it never happened, maybe it was all a dream even."

"I know, I think the same at times myself. But now my life is complete with you here in my arms Luisa. Nobody understands me, nobody thinks the way I do, nobody was raised like you and I were. Times are so different and I can't believe how lucky I was to have found you again. I only wish I did it sooner."

Luisa laughed through her tears. "I only wish I was into art! I would have found *you* instead!"

They both laughed.

"I have reservations for a really special place tonight. Do you want to take a rest or anything? We still have a few hours."

"Yes, that sounds like a great idea. I want to have enough energy for a night out on the town with you. No more dinners with a table full of others on a vineyard. Tonight it's just you and me!" Luisa looked into Giovanni's eyes with admiration. Here she was, not only with her true first love, but with someone who had made something of his passion in this ever changing world. It made her feel special.

Giovanni woke Luisa up from her nap giving her plenty of time to get ready for the evening.

They waved a cab down at the corner and headed to the restaurant. Being in the city that night reminded her a bit of her time with Samuel. Even that seemed so long ago. Those days would never compare to how she felt being there with Giovanni. He was her soul mate and aside from Michael, he was someone she felt the safest with ever since leaving California. Michael was much older now and he was busy with his own family. Giovanni could not have found her at a better time. She still could not believe it and many times she found herself staring at Giovanni, convincing herself that he was really there. He would smile at her and laugh knowing she was thinking the same thoughts that he was.

She was famished and couldn't wait to eat. The waiter gave them a quiet corner table. The restaurant was small and cozy but it was private enough for them to enjoy their alone time. It drove Giovanni crazy how some restaurants would put people so close together just to get as many reservations. He actually walked into the restaurant last week making the reservation and handed the manager extra money to be sure that their table was private enough.

After a couple of glasses of wine, Luisa started to tear up again. She seemed to be doing this a lot lately. She just couldn't believe she was sitting there with Giovanni.

"I'm so happy to be with you right now. There is a part of me though that feels guilty. For Lorenzo. I don't think he would be too happy right now seeing me with you. He was a good man, Giovanni. He really took care of me and the children."

He took her hand in his. "I do know that Luisa. I'm sorry that I upset him all those years ago. So much happened that night, I thought it out so many times in my head from days before the incident to days after. I thought back to how stupid I was to have interfered with your life and your marriage to Lorenzo. I kept thinking that if you had been married to me and another man came to us and tried to be alone with you and speak to you the way I did…it would kill me. I was wrong and I never should have disrespected Lorenzo that way." He sat back shaking his head. "You know, it's funny, I say all that and yet if I didn't do what I did and we didn't have the fight in the barn that night, the fire would not have happened and I would have went home the following morning back to my family and you would have continued on with your family. Everything would have been normal. You would have grown old with Lorenzo and neither of us would have been here. Or would we? I mean, what did happen to us that night, Luisa? Maybe it wasn't something that happened after or during the fire. Maybe it was something more powerful. Maybe we were just given a gift to have another chance at life. We will never really know. How can we? All I know is, that was a long time ago. Right now, I think that if Lorenzo was looking down he would be glad that you found someone of your own time. Please don't get upset thinking that you are doing anything

129

wrong. You surely can't live your life alone. To find someone with the same condition that will understand you is far better than being alone. We were meant to be together Luisa."

Luisa was silent as Giovanni wiped tears from her face.

"I do feel that Lorenzo is looking down happy that we found each other. I know that on his last days, he was very worried about me. He told me that I needed to be very careful and let Giuseppe, our son, take care of me. He kept apologizing that he was leaving me." She laughed at this as she wiped her own tears now. "He kept saying it was his fault and he hoped that he was not going to have to wait so long so see me again one day in eternity." Luisa held Giovanni's hand tight. "What if we never get there? What if we are stuck here forever?"

He looked at her and caressed her hand. "If that is the way it will be at least we are together my love."

The waiter came over to them bringing their meal. At first he smiled until he saw Luisa's tears and realized that he clearly interrupted an emotional discussion between the two. He silently put down their plates and asked if they needed anything else. Once he heard the answer he wished them a good meal and walked away.

The food looked and smelled so good it was a relief to get their minds off of the conversation. After finishing their meal they ordered coffee and dessert. While waiting for it to arrive, once again Giovanni took a hold of Luisa's hand on the table.

"Luisa, it's been so long since we last saw each other. This time we need to do things right. That's why I want to ask you…will you marry me?" With his other hand he exposed a diamond ring.

Luisa was speechless. At first because she was taken aback by the size of the diamond. "Oh Giovanni! You make me so happy how can I not say yes! Yes! Of course!"

He placed the ring on her finger. A couple that was not too far away was looking at them and smiling. They both nodded as if to say congratulations. Luisa smiled back at them in embarrassment.

Chapter 22

It was a warm Saturday and they decided to spend the day in Central Park. Luisa packed up some cheese, crackers and wine. It was nice to know that even after all of these years people still enjoyed spending time outdoors with family and friends. There were dogs running around catching Frisbee's, people on their bikes and many families with babies just laying out enjoying the sun.

Giovanni laid the blanket out that Luisa packed along with the food. After some wine and cheese, he laid on his back using her bag as a pillow while she used his stomach as hers.

"I still can't believe we never bumped into each other after all of these years!" she said.

Giovanni caressed Luisa's forehead, "Luisa, have you ever thought of having more children?"

She was astonished and not prepared to answer such a question, "I don't know. It's not something I ever thought about. I guess because I knew I could never really be with anyone," Luisa paused for a minute thinking hard. "I can tell you in this short time of thinking about it I don't think I could ever again have another child. Giovanni, watching all my children age, get sick and old…it is not worth the heartache."

He sighed. "Yes, I understand. I wrote letters to my children and eventually they stopped writing back. I guess I was lucky in one way not to have witnessed any of that. I'm so sorry Luisa. It was selfish of me to ask."

"Don't be silly!" she said sitting up and facing him. "I do wish things were different for you and your children." Luisa looked at him with concern knowing he regretted not being part of their lives. "Were you thinking there might be a possibility that you and I can have children? I am willing to give it a try if this is something you truly want."

He just looked at her and touched her face lightly, "Yes, I can't wait to marry you Luisa and I would love to try and have children with you. However, my concern is if it's even possible. I really wish we knew what we were dealing with here. If only there was someone we could trust. Perhaps a doctor could help. Then again, what would a doctor know? We would need someone who is more interested and

131

knowledgeable in human physics or something, maybe someone who works with lab rats!" He started to laugh.

"Wait," Luisa looked at him as if he should know what she was just thinking, "Did you say physics? I used to be friendly with someone in college who was extremely smart. That was so long ago though. Well, let's see he would be close to 60 if not already. I wanted to tell him but he was young then. He would never believe it and being he was still in school he wasn't really educated enough. Nevertheless, he was studying physics. I wonder what he did in his life. I lost touch with him, which I can say I had to do on purpose. Another horrible thing we must do in our lives. I'm sure I could look him up, I think we can trust him Giovanni."

"Ok but only on one condition," he said.

"What's that?" She sat up, curious.

"That you stop calling me Giovanni like I am some immigrant off the boat. Call me John and if you like, I will call you Louise. I think it would be better anyway. Considering when we knew each other under those names, times were not in our favor."

She gave a sarcastic smile. "Fine, *John*. I guess it would make more sense to call each other by those names in public. People who know us might find it strange."

"Ok so where do we find your old boyfriend." He sat up sipping more wine as she laughed aloud.

"Oh trust me! Nothing happened between us! I was like this in college, he was young and…well let's just say a little nerdy."

"Well I hope so, I don't want anyone near my girl!" He kissed her gently.

Luisa moved away from his kiss. "Did you forget that I said he is nearly 60 years old!"

"No I didn't forget and I know if I was 60 I would be all over you!" She just nudged him in the arm and they started to pack everything up and head back.

When they arrived at her house that evening, she started to do some research on Mitchell. It didn't take long to find him. Turned out, he had become a theoretical physicist and was running the Department of Laboratory Medicine at one of the most prestigious universities for over 20 years. She took down his information and they decided they would contact him the next day. Luisa knew instantly it was Mitchell. His picture showed that he still had the same characteristics only with grey hair and a bit of weight on him. Even in his photo he did not smile. Instead he looked more annoyed with having to take the picture at all, which made her smile as she remembered how he used to be.

The next morning she called the university. Being he was busy now, she left a message for him to call her back. Not even an hour had passed and he returned the call.

"Luisa? My goodness, how have you been? It's been so long!" He actually sounded very happy to hear from her.

"Oh, Mitchell it's so wonderful to hear from you! I can't tell you how happy I am that you remembered me! I was worried I wouldn't get a phone call back!" She was genuinely happy to hear his voice and that he was doing well with his life.

"Are you kidding me? Do you really think I could forget the only girl in college who gave me the time of day? Even if it was just as a friend." They both laughed. "So where have you been? What are you up to and where do you live?"

So many questions.

"Well, I'm teaching." Luisa stopped herself and looked up at the ceiling out of annoyance to her for the slip. It wasn't every day she talked to someone from her past. There was a pause on the other end. They both knew Luisa had about 15 years on Mitchell. "You teach. Still? Well you *do* sound great I will say that!"

Luisa knew she had to change the subject quickly, "Mitchell, I was wondering if perhaps we could meet for coffee? Actually, I see you don't work too far. I'm living on Long Island, would you like to come to my house for a visit? I would love to catch up and there is something that I would like to discuss with you. I know it seems awkward, I mean, it's been so long and everything. It's just I think you might be able to help me with something and quite frankly I feel I can trust you."

Mitchell laughed, "Well I'm glad to hear that. I would love to see you too. How about tonight?"

"That would be wonderful! I can't thank you enough Mitchell." She proceeded to give him directions to her home. Luisa purposely did not use video for this call. She needed to meet with him in person. He had to believe her this time; just looking at her was proof enough!

Later that evening Luisa had everything set up for her guest, coffee and dessert. She even put out some of the harder liquor thinking it might come in handy once Mitchell saw her and heard what they were going to tell him. When the doorbell rang her stomach felt sick with apprehension knowing how ludicrous this all sounded to any normal person. However, Mitchell was the only one who could help them. At least the only person she felt she could trust. He was much older now and wasn't sure if he would care to help them out but she assumed he would just for the fact that he of all people would be so interested to know the truth. Scientifically speaking that is.

Luisa walked over and opened the door with a warm smile at the sight of her old friend. "Hello Mitchell, it's so wonderful to see you!"

Mitchell looked at Luisa and smiled politely. "Oh, hi. I suppose your mother has told you about me? Wow, you really look just like her!" he said. He couldn't stop looking at Luisa and the resemblance between what he assumed was mother and daughter.

Luisa gestured Mitchell into the house and closed the door behind him. Giovanni walked over and put his hand out introducing himself as Luisa's friend John.

Luisa had them sit around the dining room table where the coffee and dessert was. She poured him a cup and one for herself and Giovanni as well.

"You must be told all the time how much you look like your mother. It's funny, the last time I saw her she was just about your age, too. It's amazing how DNA works." He mixed his coffee up as he spoke, "So where is she, your mother?"

Luisa looked at Giovanni. "Well, actually Mitchell, Luisa is not my mother. You see…"

Mitchell looked surprised and then cut her off. "Oh! Well, wait a minute now. Grandmother?" he laughed at his mistake. "How silly of me, I apologize for that. It's just, my son John is about your age. Oh but of course, Luisa was older than I was. You know, my son John works in the same field as I do. He works with me at the lab. I sometimes think he might be smarter than I am! But don't tell him that." Mitchell laughed finding it amusing that anyone, even his own offspring, could be smarter than he was. You could see in his eyes how proud he was of his son.

The entire time Giovanni sat back, smirking and drinking his coffee. Enjoying the show.

Luisa tried again. "Mitchell. I'm sure you don't remember this but there was a day that Luisa tried to tell you something. Something that seemed so ridiculously strange and actually impossible. Well, I guess not really impossible, eh?" she looked over at Giovanni and smiled, "She started to tell you she was born in the late 1800's and grew up in Sicily."

Mitchell looked at her confused, "We had a lot of conversations then. I never did get your name by the way."

"Luisa. My name is Luisa. Mitchell it's me. I was trying to tell you back then that something happened to me many years ago and since then I have not aged."

He slowly put his mug down while looking at her the entire time, "What is this? Is Luisa playing a joke on me? I mean you look exactly like her but I am past that. Tell her to come out now." He seemed a bit annoyed at this point. He didn't understand the humor in this. It wasn't as if they were children.

"Oh boy, how do I explain this to you?" She looked worn out already, looking up at the ceiling as if the answer was there, "Do you remember that girl you liked? Oh, what was her name? Barbara? Yes, Barbara that was it! Do you remember how she would always smile at you while we were in the cafeteria and I told you to go talk to her but you wouldn't?"

Mitchell picked up his mug and proceeded to drink from it. "Stories your mother, rather *grandmother* told you I see."

Luisa saw this was going to be harder then she expected. No story or picture would convince Mitchell. He was going to have an answer for everything.

Giovanni stepped in at this point. He told Mitchell the entire story. Afterwards he asked, "Mitchell, all we ask of you is to take a blood test. If it comes out abnormal in any way, we just want you to let us know. You don't need to believe any of this, why would you. At least do us this favor. Please, for your friend Luisa."

Mitchell looked at them both annoyed, "I'm not sure what's going on here or where Luisa is. I don't know what it is you want me to look for or why you don't go to a doctor yourselves. However, for my dear friend, who would not approve of this trick you are playing on me by the way, I will do it. After that, don't call me anymore. I just hope you would tell me if Luisa had passed. It's disrespectful to her you know." He looked right at Luisa, got up, took a card out of his wallet and threw it on the table, "Come by tomorrow at noon."

He then got up and let himself out. Luisa was upset that Mitchell was hurt. She could see in his eyes that he felt betrayed and foolish for coming. Giovanni consoled her. "Don't worry my love. If anyone will figure something out it will be him I'm sure."

Later that evening they headed to bed hopeful with the possibility that there was someone out there who could help them understand what was going on. More importantly know if it was safe enough to have a baby. If they were going to be on this earth forever, they might as well make the best of it. Together.

Chapter 23

The next afternoon Giovanni and Luisa headed to Mitchell's lab. After giving their name to someone behind a desk, a young woman came out from the back of the office and greeted them.

"Pleased to meet you, my name is Sofia and I will be assisting you today. Please follow me."

They followed her down a hallway and into a smaller room that was all white. On the counter, there were all medical instruments, needles etc.

Sofia proceeded to put gloves on and asked who would like to go first.

Luisa seemed a bit confused and asked "Won't Mr. Roth be coming in?"

"No, he asked that I do the favor for him today as he is tied up for the rest of the afternoon. If you would just have a seat here and roll your sleeve up a bit we can get started." Sofia motioned to a seat in front of them.

Luisa seemed very annoyed at this and looked at Giovanni, "I can't believe Mitchell chose not to meet us today!"

Sofia stated again, "As I mentioned, Mr. Roth…"

Luisa was quick to cut in, "No offense to you, my apologies. It's just I know Mr. Roth was not happy with a conversation we last had which just brings me to believe it was by choice that he is not here right now. Ouch."

"Sorry!" Sofia was getting nervous as she tied the rubber strap around her arm.

"Can you please tell me if Mr. Roth will be the one testing our blood work? If not I would really rather not go through with this if you don't mind." Luisa covered her arm before Sofia could take her blood.

"I will be sure to specify to Mr. Roth that only he is to do all testing if you like."

"Yes, please. This is very important. And if you could allow me to leave a note for him as well I would greatly appreciate it." Luisa smiled at Sofia and took her hand away from her arm for her to proceed.

Luisa read back the note that she wrote for Mitchell to Giovanni after Sofia had left the room giving them a minute.

"Dear Mitchell. It was disappointing to see that you were not here today to help me out with a favor I asked of you. If you truly were loyal to your dear friend Luisa, I would ask you to do at least one thing. I ask that you and only you do all testing. It is very important to me as it is to Luisa. I thank you kindly for your help with this."

She also left a phone number where he could reach her with the results. They left the building and decided to get something to eat.

***

The following week was stressful for both Luisa and Giovanni. Ever since they discussed having a baby, it seemed to be all they wanted now. The one negative thing was the possibility of it not happening. They didn't even know if Mitchell could find anything abnormal or different with their blood tests. They honestly assumed it would just show they are normal and healthy. If that were the case, they decided they would go ahead, get married and start planning their family. There was no need for them to wait it out like most couples. They waited long enough for this. There was no need to waste more time.

One evening they decided to get their minds off everything and head out to a movie. Giovanni agreed to see a romantic comedy since he's never felt as romantic as he has the last few months being with his lost love. After a fun night of going to the movies and a last minute decision on ice cream, they pulled into their driveway. As they walked up to the porch, they noticed someone sitting in a chair by the door.

"Stay here." Giovanni told Luisa after seeing there was a car parked across the street. He slowly walked up to the steps. They had forgotten to put on the front light since it was light out when they left. Giovanni could not make out who was sitting on the steps at first.

He spoke aloud, "Hi there. Can I help you with something?"

The figure got up from the chair and moved closer to the top step. It was Mitchell. He was holding a large envelope in his left hand.

"Mitchell?" Luisa started to walk closer after seeing who it was.

Mitchell walked down the steps slowly. He stopped, looked at Luisa and smiled, "Good to see you again, Luisa."

They all headed inside and as customary, Luisa served coffee with Sambuca. Both Giovanni and Luisa sat on the couch while Mitchell walked around the room, pacing with excitement.

He looked at them knowing that if he were to explain it scientifically they would be lost and confused. He tried his best to let them know what he discovered.

"I just don't know what it is. Never in all of my research have I seen anything like it! It's as if your cells are on turbo speed or something. Your cells are healing at a rapid rate. Healing instantly! Every sign of aging or wear and tear on your body must be getting healed faster than it has a chance to do any damage."

"If it's alright with you, I would like to have more tests done. I know this is exactly what you have been avoiding all of these years but you don't understand what this means to someone like me. I promise to keep this to myself. I will do all the research alone. I promise."

Luisa and Giovanni agreed that they could trust Mitchell. They were more than anxious to find out themselves what it was that happened.

"Mitchell, there is one more question we have. Luisa and I are contemplating on having a baby. Do you think this could be a problem?"

Mitchell seemed was quite for a long time. "I honestly do not know. My one concern would be that it's possible that the baby will have the same non-aging DNA make-up of the both of you. Chances would be high since its not just one of you. What if the baby is conceived and remains inside of you not growing or developing because it will never age? Or what if once the baby was born it never aged? We won't know until you try I suppose. I don't believe it would be harmful to you Luisa. I would be curious myself."

The thought of this frightened Luisa. If her baby remained inside of her what was she supposed to do? She would never have it removed yet she couldn't live that way either. Giovanni looked over at her with the same concern. All they could do was take the chance.

Mitchell got up, gave Luisa a kiss and shook Giovanni's hand. "It's getting late, I'd better get going."

Luisa felt the need to call Michael and tell him of the visit they just had. All she could really explain in her own words was that Mitchell detected something with their blood work. Their cells work rapidly to heal and cure which would explain why they haven't aged. Michael was concerned about trusting Mitchell but he did remember what good friends they once were.

That evening, Giovanni and Luisa headed to bed with an intention in mind. They were going to start the process of making a baby.

Chapter 24

Months went by. Giovanni and Luisa managed to conceive. Every week they went to Mitchell's lab for updates on the baby. Mitchell was able to get some equipment to take a sonogram. It turned out over time the baby did, in fact, start developing and growing. This was such a relief to them all. It also gave Mitchell more information to work with. He was interested in the fact that this was not passed on to the baby. He concluded it was not something that both Giovanni and Luisa were born with. It was not a trait that was carried over from generation to generation. It now made sense.

Luisa was now seven months pregnant with no complications. Not even morning sickness. Of course, they assumed it would go that way. Mitchell assured them of that. He arranged to have a midwife come to the house for when it was time to give birth. He knew that any doctor would be taking blood tests during the pregnancy and they all agreed not to take the chance.

In her first few months of pregnancy, Giovanni and Luisa got married. Since it was on such short notice, they did the best they could as far as a celebration. Money was never an issue for either of them. Over the years, they both managed to save and invest very wisely. They became experts at moving their money around, since bank accounts didn't remain open for 100 years. The party was held at one of Giovanni's favorite restaurants. Being Luisa was already pregnant, she kept the list to family and close friends only. There was no need to draw so much attention. Friends were just grateful that she finally found someone and was starting a family. If they only knew she had been through this before. Although, now it seemed like her past was all a dream. As if her life with Lorenzo never even happened. Having these feelings always made her feel guilty. Mostly due to her children. Nothing could have been worse than to see them pass on. No parent should live through that.

One Saturday, they decided to paint the extra bedroom in the house. Luisa did not want to know the sex of the baby. It seemed everyone these days found out and she still kept some of her traditional beliefs, as curious as she might have been. They painted a pale yellow room with brown accents. Giovanni did most of the work while Luisa supervised.

139

"I know this isn't something we want to think about. It's just, do you sometimes get worried that we will have to witness all of this again? I mean, our child growing old in front of our eyes. Outliving them." She looked at him with concern knowing she wasn't sure if she could go through it again.

Giovanni put down the paint roller, walked over, and took her in his arms, "My love, we need to enjoy every moment we have with this child of ours. We can't think of the future or the sadness we might encounter. Let's just be happy we were given a second chance at a life together."

Then the doorbell rang.

"I'll get it." Luisa called out.

"Are you sure? I mean you are doing all the work here, I wouldn't want you to get interrupted." He was teasing her and he managed to smile as she stuck her tongue out at him.

Giovanni continued to paint some more until he heard Luisa cry from the living room, "Giovanni!"

He dashed quickly to the other room and almost fell from shock at who he saw standing at the front door.

"Giovanni...don't be frightened." The woman walked inside towards Giovanni and put her hand on his arm, "How can you be so shocked? Look at the two of you. Did you think it possible that I too could be walking the earth for all these years?"

Luisa rushed over to hold Giovanni who still seemed to be spooked and looked over at the elderly woman, "What have you done to us! Where have you been all this time? How could you leave us? To be lost not understanding any of this!"

Giovanni stopped Luisa, "Please just stop. STOP!" He needed to think for a moment and catch his breath.

He then proceeded to walk into the kitchen leaving the two women standing there. It was Rosa, Giovanni's grandmother. She walked over to a single chair in the living room and motioned to it, "May I?"

"Yes, of course." Luisa then felt guilty for yelling at her but the shock was too much.

Giovanni came in with a bottle of scotch and two glasses. He didn't say a word. He poured scotch in his glass and sat down taking one long gulp. He then looked at Rosa and Luisa who knew not to say a word until he spoke first. "Start talking," he said.

At first, Rosa looked nervous but then she laughed, "This is too familiar."

"Excuse me?" Giovanni now looked annoyed, "The night of the fire, nonna. Tell me what happened."

Rosa looked confused, "I'm not even sure where to begin."

Luisa felt awkward. The one thing she did remember about Giovanni's grandmother was that the woman hardly spoke at all. All she ever did was nod and smile and here she was talking perfect English. Granted she had many years to learn every language she could. Luisa had actually learned how to speak French and Spanish, although their similarities with Italian had made it easy.

Giovanni took another sip. "How about you start from the night of the fire?"

"But you see, if I start from there nothing will make sense. I need to start from the beginning. Although, the beginning? Where *is* the beginning?" She seemed to be getting more and more confused as she put her hand on her cheek and Luisa couldn't help feeling sympathetic. Rosa was an elderly woman after all who now suddenly seemed very sweet, but also frightened.

"Giovanni, let's give her a moment. You have to remember that this is all very overwhelming for her as well. She hasn't seen you in so long. And she has probably been alone all these years as well." Luisa turned to her. "How about you start with the time you came to my vineyard, with Giovanni and his father? The first time you came."

Rosa reached for the glass of scotch and poured herself some. She then closed her eyes and took a slow sip. It seemed to make her more relaxed. "Ok, yes. Well if you will, I would like to go back a little further. Giovanni, do you remember when I first came to your house? It was less than a year before going to Luisa's vineyard. You had never even met me before. I lived with a cousin of your father's. I was your father's grandmother. He said he didn't remember me much, saw me when he was a little boy. But he welcomed me into his home and treated me wonderfully." She smiled at her memory.

"What I am about to tell you might sound very strange. Then again, if there are any two people who will believe the impossible it will be the two of you. Giovanni…" she paused. "I'm not really your father's grandmother."

Luisa looked down at the floor knowing Giovanni would not take this lightly. He moved to the edge of the chair, "Excuse me? What is it you are telling me? If you are not her then why would you ever come to my family?"

She put her glass back on the table getting nervous again. "I wrote a letter to your father claiming to be his grandmother. I knew that you never kept in touch with that family. You told me this yourself."

141

His eyes widened. "I told you this myself? If I never met you before how could I have told you this?"

She ignored him and continued, "I came to your house today knowing it was almost time."

"Time for what?" he asked.

She snapped at him, "If you are going to keep interrupting me how can I tell you everything?"

Giovanni and Luisa exchanged glances and they sat back and listened this time.

"It was 1902. I knew the year that I needed to come live with you and your family. There was no turning back. I wrote the letter to your father and he met me not too far from your home where I arrived on my own horse. He couldn't believe nobody dropped me off but I told him I was a strong enough woman. I didn't talk very much when I arrived. I was scared, if you want the truth. I kept to myself, helped with chores and that was it. When your father was planning the trip to Luisa's vineyard, I told him I wanted to go. Everyone thought it would be nice for me to help.

"When we arrived at the vineyard, I sat back and observed. Did what I was asked of which wasn't much. I noticed the way you both looked at each other. It was obvious to me how in love you two once were. I couldn't believe nobody else noticed. Although I did hear some of the women say things. They thought it was cute. The budding romance.

"The night of the fire so much happened. I knew I had to be on top of everything. I couldn't mess anything up. I was so nervous when I saw everyone running around looking for Luisa. I couldn't find either one of you at first. Then I saw a bunch of men had pulled both of you out. They took Luisa inside as we surrounded Giovanni. I did what I had to in a very short time, hoping nobody would notice what I was doing. I realized Giovanni that you were not conscious enough to swallow the pill I had. Thankfully, it was coated so that it would melt away and it was very tiny. I placed it in your mouth and forced water down your throat. There were buckets everywhere. I just scooped it up into my hands. Of course, I was told to stop. Having you drink water wasn't going to help they kept saying and that I could do more harm by choking you. It was enough to melt the pill and get it into your system. I left as they continued to work on you. That is when I headed inside to Luisa. Everyone was crying. I yelled at one of the women to get me water and then told them all to go away. Everyone assumed Luisa was already dead. I knew I had little time to do what was needed. I did the same to Luisa that I did to you. I had no idea if any of it would work but I assumed that if I was still standing there, it had to have worked.

I told Lorenzo that Luisa would be fine and to let her rest. They all looked at me as if I was crazy. As I walked outside back to where you were I could hear in the background the tears and screams of joy that Luisa had still been breathing. I closed my eyes in relief. Giovanni, you were already in the wagon. I was instructed to quickly get my things ready and that we were heading home immediately. It was then they told me you did not make it. It couldn't be possible though. After receiving help from one of the women to gather my stuff, I got in the wagon to head home. When I got in, I looked down at you and your father told me you would be ok and that it was a miracle. The second we got back home, I took the last pill I had on me.

I stayed at the house for a few months to make sure you recovered. It was then I knew I had to leave. I told everyone I already wrote their cousin because I wanted to go back and that I missed it there. I paid someone to come retrieve me, no questions asked. After two months I had a note written to Giovanni's father explaining my sudden death. I was old after all so it would have been of no surprise."

Giovanni looked at Rosa intensely. "You have not explained your reasoning for doing what you did. Besides the fact that I would love to know more about this pill you gave us. My question first is why did you do it? Why did you need to give it to us? Why would you care enough if you are not even my grandmother?"

Rosa knew what she was about to say was going to shock them both. She took a deep breath and said it anyway, her breath rushed. "Giovanni, Luisa. This will shock you a bit I'm sure." she paused. "I am your daughter."

Luisa touched her stomach at hearing this and Giovanni looked over at Luisa stunned.

Rosa continued, "This is very hard to explain to you. The year I come from, after years of research, time travel had been discovered. If you go, you cannot return though. Growing up, you both explained to me what it is I needed to do. I worked with John, Mitchell's son, and his team once I graduated college. We opened our own laboratory and research center. You both managed to do well for yourselves and with the help of Mitchell, we were able to do it. After he passed on, his son and I remained as head of the division. You told me when the time was that I was to come see you both. I couldn't come sooner for fear that you would never meet the way it was meant to be and I needed to be sure you already conceived me." She looked down at Luisa's belly.

143

"Years ago we could never have done this. I know this is a lot for the both of you to digest."

Luisa started to cry. They were both in shock and yet could not stop staring at Rosa. Their daughter? It seemed impossible. Then again, nothing was impossible to them. After the life they led how could they not believe any of this? It really was a lot of information to take on. Luisa stopped and held her stomach. They were having a girl. They were still confused about how they got to where they did. What was the pill that was given to them?

"Rosa, the pill. What was that?" Giovanni needed to know the answers to it all. There were so many years of wondering.

Rosa looked at them both unable to speak. She knew it sounded crazy but so far what didn't?

"The *pill*. Well it's amazing when you think about it. John was able to come up with this because of the two of you. He tested your DNA and somehow over time, he managed to figure it all out. He knew that this was a tremendous breakthrough. He knew that many people would pay anything to get their hands on this. He didn't even share this with our other colleagues. He made himself crazy for months on what to do with this information. He realized if this got out to the public, it could cause problems for the world. If millions stayed on the earth double the amount of time, we could easily run out of resources. There would be an overflow of humanity. He did not want to be responsible for that destruction. We both agreed not to try to change what God created. This had to be top secret. John made me promise not to take advantage and explained what it was that had to be done. He was so much older and wiser than I was. I promised I would do what was necessary. It seemed like such a waste of research in a way. He thought long and hard and finally decided that he could manipulate the drug. Perhaps not use it to the fullest extent but a drug with one eighth of the potential might be able to cure cancer. A cure for cancer! He knew what he needed to do. He tested it repeatedly until it finally worked. He became a legend. It was then that I told him about me. About the time travel and how it was his discovery that I gave to the two of you that night. John realized at that moment why it needed to come natural and the sole purpose of this discovery drug in its fullest extent was really for the benefit of the three of us only and by doing that lead you both to his father therefore ending up with the cure." Rosa was looking to the side and reminiscing how proud she was to be a part of all of this, "Don't you see? It was because of the two of you there was a cure for cancer!"

144

Both Giovanni and Luisa took a breather. They looked at each other. It was clear Giovanni was thinking long and hard about this, "But this doesn't make any sense. So, you are telling me the only reason we lived longer is because of a drug that was invented due to us living longer. Think about what I am saying here! It's one big circle!" He looked at Rosa waiting for an answer.

"I understand. Believe me, it has driven us crazy ever since. One is a result of the other, which is a result of the first. You will drive yourself crazy just trying to figure it all out. But the bottom line is that it is what it is." Rosa sat back with a feeling of relief that she finally was able to share this with someone and it was all over now. Her mission was complete. "Listen, I have lived even longer on this earth than the both of you. It wasn't easy for me to do. I had lived a life with the two of you already. Then I had to do it all over again. Only this time I had to live a lifestyle that was very difficult. No electronics like the ones we have nowadays. It was very hard to adjust to farm life. If I didn't come back, the both of you would have died in that fire and I would never have existed. All those people that were cured of such a terrible sickness were able to survive. I waited and waited until the discovery of time travel came about. The second I heard it was being worked on, I knew what must be done. I knew the age I was going also. Thankfully I had an in with the researchers due to all my involvement over time. They were looking for volunteers within so I offered."

Luisa got up to walk around a bit. So much information was given to her, it was hard to remember it all. She started going through everything she was just told. Then something came to mind. "Rosa?" She stopped and looked at her as if she just realized something major, "You didn't really mention Giovanni and I much during your years working with Mitchell's son."

Rosa's emotion changed. She knew this question was coming and was surprised it didn't come sooner, "I cannot and will not reveal anything about your future. I was instructed to tell you what I did so that you would educate me as I grew up. That was it." At that, she got up and headed to the door, "I need to go now."

Giovanni stood up quickly, "You can't go! You have to stay with us! After all you are our..." Giovanni said the next word as if it sounded strange, "daughter."

Walking towards them, she hugged both Giovanni and Luisa, "I will see you again. Very soon." She opened the door and stopped herself, looking worried, "Remember, you cannot tell Mitchell any of this. His son told me if they know it will only interfere with the research. It must come naturally. It's very important." They agreed to keep it to themselves.

Chapter 25

Luisa was about two weeks away from her due date. They didn't do much lately, just stayed home a lot. The baby was being born during the summer and it was too hot to do anything. She already told her school that she would not be returning. Giovanni had invested enough money over time that they could live comfortably without working for the moment. Luisa was disappointed that she could not return to school in September, she enjoyed the work. It gave her something to do every day but now that she was having a baby, she would be busy enough. One afternoon after lunch, the doorbell rang. Giovanni opened the door to find Rosa standing there. She looked very concerned but managed a smile.

Giovanni was thrilled to see her, "Rosa! Come in! We were worried we would never see you again. Like this I mean... I can't believe I let you leave that night without getting your information. I really wish you stayed with us."

Rosa walked in holding her small clutch bag. She was greeted then by Luisa who gave her a hug, "Thank God you returned," was all Luisa could manage to say through tears. She seemed to be a bit more emotional these days.

After about an hour of chatting, Rosa asked if it would be ok to take a nap. They never discussed anything other than current times. They knew how Rosa refused to tell them anything even though they had so many questions.

Luisa took her to the guest room and asked her to consider staying with them for a while. Rosa would not even tell them where she had been staying or living all these years.

Rosa smiled at her, "I'll think about it." She then headed to the bedroom to nap.

About three hours later, Luisa started to feel cramping in her lower abdomen. She ignored it at first and did not tell Giovanni until she noticed the pain came every half an hour like clockwork.

"Giovanni? I think the baby is coming." She looked at him with fear, although she wasn't sure why, she had three children before. Or was that just a dream? It sure seemed like it.

He called Mitchell and the midwife. They were both at the house in twenty minutes. Giovanni decided to wake Rosa but she was too tired. She just smiled and took his hand in hers squeezing tight, "I'm really tired right now, Giovanni."

He told Mitchell that Rosa was a relative of Michael's wife who was staying for a couple of days with them.

Giovanni wanted to help Luisa so he focused more on the baby and let Rosa sleep.

Not even two hours passed and you could hear the sound of a baby crying. The midwife cleaned up the baby girl and handed her to Luisa after first taking all her vitals. Mitchell went to the other room to let the older woman know everything was all right.

Giovanni and Luisa were thrilled with their new daughter.

"She is so beautiful. Just like her mother." Giovanni kissed Luisa on the forehead.

Mitchell returned to the bedroom where Luisa gave birth. "Giovanni, can I see you for a moment?" He walked into the other room.

"What is it? You look upset. You said we shouldn't have a problem with the baby! Please do not tell me things have changed." Worried, Giovanni followed Mitchell into the hallway.

Mitchell shook his head, "No. No, the baby looks healthy. I will check her again in a moment to be sure. Giovanni, the relative staying with you, she's not breathing. She's dead."

Giovanni looked at him in astonishment. He quickly ran to the room where Rosa had been sleeping. Shaking her lightly and calling her name it was obvious Mitchell was right.

"I'm sorry for your loss. So ironic that life just emerged at the same time another was lost." Mitchell stood in the doorway, "I will take care of this. Giovanni go back to your baby. Your relative was elderly. She couldn't have gone any better than the way she did." Mitchell started to walk away but turned to look at him, "Do you want me to call Michael?"

The words that Mitchell said hit Giovanni. One life starts while another ends. It had to be because of the birth. It made some sort of sense. There could not have been two of them on this planet during the same time. It had to be the reason. He needed to tell Luisa.

"No, that's ok. I'm sure Luisa will want to call him. Thank you Mitchell, for everything."

148

Chapter 26

The following several months went by. Giovanni and Luisa enjoyed their new baby daughter. They mourned the loss of her future self as well. After all of these years, Luisa was still not used to losing a loved one. Although she did not know the elderly Rosa, knowing her significance, it still hurt. Luisa had been there for all of her children during their last days. She stood by their sides, each one of them and had to witness their passing stricken with grief and guilt. As she looked at her new little baby Rosa, she knew it she would probably have to go through the same ordeal again, the same pain and anguish.

One morning after her daily morning routine, Luisa looked at herself in the mirror. She had to stop and really stare at herself for a moment. Something didn't seem the same. She could not pinpoint it. Maybe it was just from being tired taking care of little Rosa. It had been a long time since Luisa was getting up in the middle of the night for feedings.

****

They enjoyed their days with Rosa at the park or the beach. One day they were having lunch on a blanket watching Rosa looking at the trees move in the wind. Every time the wind blew, her head would move around as if trying to catch something. They found this very amusing to watch.

"I don't know about you but I've never felt so tired lately. I guess this is the first time I was really involved with taking care of a baby." Giovanni regretted the life he had with his children back in Italy. He always felt he wasn't a good father to them. When he realized he wasn't aging knew he could not just walk back into their lives without questions being asked. In a way he found it ironic that because of his daughter Rosa, he missed so much with his other children but he would not blame her for that at all. Rosa was a miracle and without her, he would never have ended up with his true love. He considered himself lucky. Most people are not given such an option.

Luisa laughed, "It's funny you say that because the other morning I was thinking the same thing. Also, if you look closely I think I might be getting wrinkles under my eyes!" She put her face close to Giovanni for him to look at her newly found eye wrinkles.

"Stop. You do not have wrinkles. You are more beautiful than ever." Kissing the sides of her eyes. Then he started to wonder more about what they were both saying. If he was feeling tired and Luisa was seeing wrinkles, could it be possible that maybe they were starting to actually age?

"Do you ever think that maybe one day we will get old?" He watched Rosa in her carrying chair the entire time as he touched her little fingers.

"Yes I think about it every day. I'm scared one morning I might wake up a little old woman. I can't tell you how many dreams I've had over time of that actually happening. Why? Are you worried?" Luisa looked at Giovanni with concern.

He continued to look at Rosa, "No. It's just all these years we both, at least I know I did, hope to age like everyone else and move on. Now, we have Rosa. Everything is different. I don't want to go anywhere. I just want to be with you and her. All these years I finally got what I wanted. It would be a shame not to enjoy it." He then looked at Luisa and leaned in to give her a kiss on the lips, "Why don't we give Mitchell a call later? He's been making us draw blood every week now for more testing. I just want to see if he came up with anything interesting. Remember what Rosa said? He would make a great discovery. As tired as I am of being pricked we can't let him down." They both laughed and agreed to get in touch with him that evening.

After dinner, Luisa put Rosa in her crib. They both video called Mitchell but there was no answer. Within half an hour, Mitchell was at their front door.

"Sorry for not calling. When something is on my mind I just have to head out and share it with you two."

They all sat around the table.

"What is it? Is everything ok?" Luisa asked as she brought out coffee mugs.

Mitchell made a cup, "Oh yes. Actually, it's very ok. Quite amazing actually. You see, I've been comparing all your tests to see if there is a change or a pattern that I need to follow. I'm working on two different things. I know you gave me your consent to experiment. I've been fooling around with different research strategies and I think I might have come up with something. I'm not sure yet but I'm working on it. I used the structure in your DNA to come up with the possibility of creating a medicine to keep us from aging. So far, what I have, is working with lab rats. I give them a virus, no worries, nothing deadly. After administering what I came up with again, using your structure, I was able to witness the rats instantly curing themselves of this virus."

Mitchell looked at them as if he discovered the wheel. He seemed so proud but more so he seemed shocked that something like this could even work.

He then looked at them both, "The possibility of this is remarkable. It would be an amazing breakthrough. I just don't know how to go about anything like this. I mean, how would I even begin to explain. There is still so much that needs to be done. I just thought you two should know. So much good can come out of this." He smiled which indicated to them that it was not that he was proud of himself but more grateful to them for trusting him with all of this.

Then his face changed to worry. "There is, however, something else I also noticed. The rate your cells are healing and moving around has slowed down a bit. It's not a dramatic difference but indeed, it has slowed. Now, have you noticed anything different? Aches, memory loss? Anything that a normal person would feel as they got older, not that you would know." He rolled his eyes.

Giovanni put a hand through his hair, "I knew it. I knew everything was too good to be true. Just today we were talking about this. Now with Rosa here and finally I am with Luisa. It's all going to end isn't it?" He got up from his chair in panic.

"Giovanni wait, that is not what Mitchell is saying." Luisa looked back at Mitchell. "Is it?"

"There is no need for alarm now. We will just monitor everything a little more frequently. Just be sure to tell me when you notice anything is all. Giovanni, there is nothing to worry about. I just want to be on top of things. For the first time, I don't know what I'm dealing with here. I have no assistance from anyone, which actually brings me to another question. Would you be against me bringing my son into this? He's trained as I was and I know I can trust him. He's not about making money or the fame from it. He is truly interested in research alone. I won't involve him unless you give me the blessing."

Both Luisa and Giovanni looked at each other knowing they were thinking the same thing, remembering what Rosa said to them. Mitchell had involved his son in this discovery. His son John worked with Rosa in all of this. The secret of their main discovery stayed with only the two of them. They also remembered that Rosa said neither Mitchell nor his son could know this right now. It could change everything.

They gave Mitchell the blessing to involve his son, anything to help. After Mitchell left, Giovanni and Luisa remained at the table to continue the conversation.

151

It was upsetting Luisa that she could not share information with Mitchell. She wanted to, thinking that maybe it would make things easier for him if he knew the steps he needed to take, "What do you think would happen if we did tell Mitchell all about Rosa and what she told us? It's not that he wouldn't believe us. This way nothing can go wrong."

Giovanni shook his head fiercely. "No Luisa! We must not tell him. We are faced with something we know absolutely nothing about! It's not every day that people live as long as we do at the age we do! For heaven's sake, what about Rosa and this whole time travel? People would only laugh at us if they knew. It's the unknown Luisa. We can't mess with that. What if by telling him, everything changes and goes wrong. We don't even know if this breakthrough might have something to do with the time travel. Then what? We die in that fire that's what!"

Luisa cut him off, "No that can't be. We are here. No matter what, everything that happened already happened or it would have happened already!" She said, confused. "My point is Rosa is real. She is a baby now but we saw her ourselves in the future! So are you saying that if one thing doesn't go the same we will just disappear? What about all the lives we touched? Wouldn't all of that be affected as well? Life cannot just change so easily."

Giovanni seemed confused as well, "I don't know. What about Parallel Universes, the theory that every 'what if' actually takes place only in other universes. What if we are living one right now and if we died in that fire its just another universe that went on. Luisa I don't know, I'm not a scientist. Rosa knew more than we do working with Mitchell's son and if she said to keep our mouth shut then that is what we are going to do. Understood?"

They both agreed to stay quiet.

Chapter 27

Mitchell agreed to meet Luisa and Giovanni at their house for lunch. It was a last minute invitation but he heard concern in their voices.

When he arrived, he could see what their concern was immediately. He could see it in their faces. They seemed to be aging dramatically and not at a normal pace. Rosa was close to two years old now and it seemed that Giovanni and Luisa had aged about ten years. The most obvious was the wrinkles around their eyes, the skin on their face, which seemed to sag more by the chin and the grey hair that seemed to have come out of nowhere.

"Is this it? Is this how it's going to be?" Luisa was in a panic. "I mean, I just had a baby! What will happen to Rosa if we are not here to raise her?"

Mitchell was speechless at first and thought quickly as he walked inside. "Now calm down Luisa. We will figure this out. It had to happen eventually. We just couldn't have known when or at what pace. Let me do some more tests and I will work all night on it. I'm sure I could see the timing of things."

Giovanni was quiet as he sat on the edge of the couch with his hands at his face. Mitchell could see the concern in his eyes. "Don't worry Giovanni, we will figure things out."

Their main concern was for their daughter. They already discussed the possibility of asking Mitchell to take care of her if something were to happen. Part of them did not want to think of that. They needed to take things day by day and not waste whatever precious time they did have with Rosa worrying the worst.

After two weeks of daily blood tests, Mitchell met up with them at the lab to discuss what he had come up with after running numerous tests.

"It appears the cells are not healing as quickly as they used to. I compared each day's progress to the prior day and over the two-week period; I came up with the pace at what we are looking at here. It's hard to make an assumption right now. We need more time to test. I know it's a lot to ask but I have a kit here for you to take home. This way you can test yourselves every day. I will get it at the end of the week or you can drop it off. We'll examine things over a month, two months, whatever it takes. I need to see a pattern. Just a little longer. In the

153

meantime, please just live your life like you normally would. Don't let this interfere. It could even cause more damage for all we know so just go on as you always have."

They agreed to do what Mitchell told them and took samples daily of their blood. Luisa went out and bought a dye for her hair so things did not look too different too soon. Rosa kept them busy so it was easy to take each day as Mitchell suggested. They knew that they were already blessed, considering all factors. However things might turn out, Rosa would be fine. The older version of her never showed that she lost them at an early age. In fact, Giovanni recalled something she had said when she first arrived back at their house about things seeming familiar. He assured Luisa that Rosa had to have been old enough to remember which meant they would be fine.

Death was something they invited in the past. It got to a point that they both went through times where it was all they ever wanted. For the first time death seemed a frightening event. They were finally faced with the possibility and were not sure exactly how to handle it. It was the unknown timing that got them.

Chapter 28

Rosa was growing up fast. She kept both Luisa and Giovanni busy enough. They signed her up for all the classes that were offered for children her age.

They taught Rosa to speak Italian as well as English, and hoped that one day it would come in handy. When she was three years old they took her to Sicily. They rented a villa on the water and stayed for two weeks.

Rosa loved playing in the sand on the beach and they loved watching her.

"What if we just moved here for good. I mean why not? We don't have jobs anymore in New York. We could move here before Rosa starts school even." Luisa said as she put a hat on Rosa. The little girl laughed and took it right off throwing it on the floor. "Ugh, stubborn little girl."

"Luisa, you know very well we can't do that. Rosa never said anything about living in Italy. We need to keep in contact with Mitchell and John. If we live here it could change everything."

"What if that *was* the plan and we just don't know. What if we do live in Italy and return to America one day when Rosa is older."

"I think she would have told us to do that. Something tells me we need to stay local, close to Mitchell and that's what we need to do."

Luisa was irritated with Giovanni's persistence. Who was he to make all the final decisions?

Giovanni looked over at her. "I'll tell you what? Why don't we buy a villa like this one that we can call our own and visit every summer?"

Luisa managed a smile.

Chapter 29

The time came when Rosa turned old enough for Giovanni and Luisa to start explaining things to her. It was her thirteenth birthday. Weeks leading up to her big day, Rosa told them what she would like to do to celebrate her birthday that year. Of course it involved her friends, which they both approved of. She asked to have a sleepover with five girls. Giovanni jokingly asked if it would be ok for him to sleep somewhere else that evening knowing how loud it can get with six teenage girls up all night. Luisa wouldn't hear of it. She needed the support herself in case things got out of hand or someone had to run out to get something at the store.

At this point, both Giovanni and Luisa had aged a bit. They appeared to have aged around 20 years even though only 10 years had passed. Giovanni had grey hair on the sides of his head, which Luisa said she liked. It made him look distinguished. Luisa on the other hand, colored her hair frequently. She was not liking the grey look on her at all. The wrinkles also deepened and multiplied, which was strange for them to see happen so rapidly along with the body aches. They were starting to realize they didn't appreciate the gift they were given enough. Getting old was not easy.

Rosa was excited about her birthday arriving. She was finally going to be a teenager and she hoped that her parents would start treating her like one instead of being so protective of her. They always wanted to know where she was and who she was with at all times. It was starting to get to her since the other parents didn't act that way towards their children. They always told her they had their reasons but it still annoyed Rosa.

Giovanni and Luisa decided they would have a talk with Rosa the week following her birthday. No need to freak her out for her sleepover.

A week after her party, Luisa made Rosa's favorite dinner. Towards the end of the meal she looked over at Giovanni and he gave her a nod which was the sign that they would begin talking to her about what her future had in store for her.

Luisa was very nervous about this. She felt bad for Rosa and wanted her to live a normal life like all the other girls her age. Once this was told to her she could either regard her parents as certifiably insane or she would stress knowing the obligation she holds. Either

156

way, things would not be the same. They decided that thirteen was a good age to start telling her. This way she could start taking the necessary classes in school to prepare herself for college and what she would major in. They felt she should be familiar with what it was she would be doing with her life as early as possible.

Luisa cleared her voice. "Rosa, there is something daddy and I would like to talk to you about."

Rosa stopped playing with her food and without moving her head her eyes looked up at Luisa and then over to Giovanni who just gave a crooked smile as if he was guilty of something.

"What is this about? Listen, if you are going to start talking about *growing up stuff*, please don't. It's bad enough we have to hear this stuff in school. I'm not going to sit here and discuss it with my parents!"

Giovanni laughed, "No, nothing like that I promise. It's just, we need to tell you about our past, *our* past that is." He moved a finger between Luisa and himself.

"Oh my God were you in trouble or in jail?" Rosa demanded.

"Would you stop and let us talk!" Luisa shook her head in annoyance. They thought about how they would start this conversation. It reminded Luisa of when she and Lorenzo had to tell their children so long ago. For some reason it seemed much easier then. Back then, the children didn't question as much but she knew that in today's age, Rosa would never in a million years believe the story.

"We have something very extraordinary to tell you. Truth is you won't believe it. Most importantly you cannot, under any circumstances, tell anyone about what we are about to tell you. Do you understand?" Giovanni put his strict voice on.

"Geez, what is it? You two are making me nervous." Rosa had the attitude of a typical teenager now, that was for sure.

Luisa spoke first. "One night, a very long time ago, your father and I were in an accident. It was a fire. Both of us should have died that night but we didn't. Someone did something to us to save our lives. But in doing so, they gave us something that changed who we were. I mean, not so much who we were but gave us a gift if you would." Luisa looked over at Giovanni for assistance hoping he would take over, she couldn't find the right words.

Giovanni proceeded. "Rosa, your mother and I were really born in the late 1800's. In that fire, an elderly woman, claiming to be my grandmother, administered a pill to us both. That pill had the power to keep us from aging. We remained the same age physically since 1902. I know that this is not something we expect you to believe right

157

away, it sounds ludicrous; I know that. But somehow you have to try to understand this. The reason we are telling you is because that woman, my grandmother...well...that woman was you. When you are older, much older, time travel will be discovered and you will be one of the first to use it. You saved our lives Rosa and its up to you to save many more. The thing is, Mitchell and John know about your mother and I. They have been testing on us for many years now. Mitchell didn't believe us either until he took our blood. Mitchell actually went to college with your mother when he was only 18 years old."

Rosa looked at them both like they were out of their minds. "Is this some sort of joke?" She started to look around for a hidden camera with a smile of excitement on her face. At this reaction Giovanni sighed hanging his head low in defeat. It was hard enough explaining this to anyone but to explain it to a teenage girl seemed to be an impossible undertaking.

"Rosa, pay attention, this is no joke!" Luisa snapped. She got up and went into her bedroom and returned with a box. She placed it on the table and opened it up. One by one she took out photos, ID cards and all her memories from over the years that were important enough to keep for this day. Rosa wasn't used to seeing photo's like that. People carried around a card, which held all the photos organized on a small screen. The only time people would print them out was to put in frames around the house. Even then those were rare but when they were printed the image appeared lifelike in 3D, unlike these photos.

Rosa started looking at them all. She especially looked at the photos that were clearly taken long ago. They were black and white, similar to the ones she saw in the history programs at school. You can see that it wasn't from recent times and even though it was very possible now a days to photo shop anything with a computer, something inside her told her that this was not the work of a computer program. It gave her the chills seeing the faces from so long ago along with her mother standing right there next to that family. The family was Lorenzo and the children.

"Mommy, stop this. I don't like you talking this way and I'm getting scared." Rosa was close to tears and couldn't understand what was going on. She always figured her parents to be pretty normal smart folk. Where was all of this coming from? She couldn't understand it and didn't want to. She wanted to get up and leave.

"Rosa, honey, we are not trying to scare you. You have to know because this is a big part of your future." She then handed her daughter another photo. It was of an elderly woman sitting in a rocking chair with a blanket on her legs surrounded by children. The woman had no smile.

"Are you saying this is me?" Rosa looked closely at the photo. As she got closer she really tried to examine the woman's face. Something struck her and she saw her own eyes looking back at her and dropped the photo instantly. "This can't be me, it doesn't make sense! If this photo is so old why am I old?"

"We told you, you returned from the future." Giovanni knew how insane it all sounded just hearing it himself.

Rosa just looked at him. "Why are you telling me this?"

"We need to tell you. Sweetheart, this is going to sound even crazier. Right before you were born, your older self came to visit us. She...I mean you, told us everything that happened. You even said we needed to tell you around this time. I just wish you told us how it went." Giovanni looked away shaking his head at how difficult this was. "You also took this pill after giving it to your mother and I. I assumed you were my grandmother years ago and that you passed away. But you said you couldn't approach us. Oh Rosa, there is so much to tell I'm starting to confuse myself even." Giovanni got up, clearly upset.

Luisa tried to relieve him. She placed her hands on his shoulders and turned to Rosa. "How about we tell you as much as we know and you can ask whatever questions you like? I'm sure you will have plenty. Apparently, with John doing all this research on your father and I, he managed to discover a cure for cancer using our DNA make-up. I couldn't explain how to you, I never really understood all of that but the point is that he did. So basically, it's like a circle. You could say your life is just beginning. From here, you grow old and work alongside John and his team. Once you reach a certain age, you return to the past using a time machine which you would not tell us anything about. Very little was told to us Rosa for fear of things not coming natural. Most importantly is that you stressed to us we could not tell Mitchell or John any of this. All of what happens must come naturally. Now, once you go back you need to take a pill yourself, which means you will also be around for a very long time."

Rosa's eyes widened from fear. "I can't do this. If this is real, which I still don't see how it is, mommy I can't do this. I'm scared!" She started to bite her nail.

Giovanni got up and hugged his daughter. "Sweetheart you will be much older then and confident. We are telling you now so that you take this path in your life as far as school is concerned. Mitchell and John are coming over tonight to talk to you more."

Rosa looked up at Giovanni. "Is my 'older self' still around?"

Giovanni looked over at Luisa. Her face showed what the answer to that question was. Rosa started to cry and got up and ran into her bedroom.

They did not go after her knowing all of this would be a shock if she even believed it. Rosa didn't come out of her room for an hour after speaking with her parents. Giovanni knocked on her door a couple of times reminding her not to speak with her friends about their conversation but she never even answered him.

Mitchell and John arrived, providing a little relief to Luisa. John was around the same age that Giovanni and Luisa appeared. He was in his fifties and Mitchell was much older, barely able to walk. He had a walker with him. John was more in charge of everything now concerning Luisa and Giovanni, with Mitchell on the sidelines.

"Well, you knew this was the way it was going to go." John tried to reassure Luisa.

"Perhaps we should have waited until she was older. She's too young to understand anything like this, what were we thinking?" Luisa had tears streaming down her face.

Giovanni wiped them for her. "She has to find out sooner or later. We wanted her to know so that she can be prepared."

"I still don't see why you even had to tell her if you ask me but you already knew how I felt." John was not in agreement with telling Rosa. He did not know the entire story about Luisa traveling back. They were not even going to tell John and Mitchell their plan to tell Rosa but knew without proof from them scientifically, Rosa would never believe them.

"I'll go tell Rosa you are here." She headed towards Rosa's bedroom and knocked on the door. "Rosa, honey? John and Mitchell are here, can you please come out and say hi to them?"

A few minutes later the door opened and Rosa stepped out. Luisa whispered to her, "Remember, you mustn't tell them about your older self. They only know about daddy and I."

She headed for the living room and went over to give Mitchell and John a hug. She had grown up with them always around and regarded them as family. She then sat down facing them both while Luisa and Giovanni stood close by.

"Do you know what they have been telling me? I'm really worried about them." Rosa was being very serious and in no way joking. Her eyes were starting to well up with tears again.

John sat closer to the edge of the couch. "Rosa, I know this is an insane thought. You never hear of this, only in silly movies, right?

Well, your parents aren't telling you they are vampires. They are just saying that something happened to them. Now, you know I'm a man of science and speaking as a scientist and a very renowned one I might add, they are telling the truth. We have been testing their DNA and blood structure. I've never seen anything like it before. If you like you can all come to the lab one day and I will show you normal cells verses your parents and explain to you the difference and it will prove what they are telling you is the truth."

"I think you all have gone crazy." Rosa folded her arms and sat back looking at the floor in anger.

Mitchell now spoke. "Rosa. Is it crazy? Yes, it is. Can it happen? Yes, it can. It doesn't really matter if you believe them or not right now. You will see it all come together in your lifetime. There is nothing you need to do right now except enjoy your youth. Be a teenager, get in trouble - "

Giovanni quickly looked at him. "Hey!"

"Sorry, but you know what I'm trying to say, right Rosa? Your parents didn't have to share this with you. They wanted to because they want to be honest with you about everything, that's all. There is nothing to be worried about. As John said, come by the lab one day with your parents. We'll show you around and explain further."

Rosa seemed a little more relaxed. What Mitchell said was right in a way. Right now she didn't have to worry about anything and she didn't have to believe them at all. If it's all true then she will find out one day. In the meantime, she can pretend that tonight never even happened.

Rosa mumbled, "Thanks Mitchell."

Mitchell looked over to Luisa. "Got any coffee?"

Chapter 30

Rosa walked into the kitchen one morning to grab something for breakfast. Luisa was always up before her and ready to make Rosa anything she wanted. That morning though, Luisa was still in bed. Surprised at this, Rosa looked around the living room and then headed into her parents' bedroom where she saw Luisa still in bed. Her father had already gotten up early and headed out for his early run. She walked over to where Luisa was laying and tapped her on the shoulder gently.

"Mama? Are you ok?" Rosa felt bad waking her up but needed to be sure she was fine. The last year had been strange for her ever since she was told her how long her parents had been around, and that Rosa would be traveling back in time one day to make that happen. She wasn't sure anymore what she could wake up to on any given day. Before, everything was so good and so normal. Ever since telling Rosa, her parents seemed to think it was fun to tell her stories of their past. There were many stories to be told. Most of the time Rosa would make an excuse up that she had to finish some homework just so she didn't have to hear another story. She heard enough.

Luisa slowly opened her eyes to see her daughter standing over her. Startled at first she jumped up. "Oh, Rosa! What time is it? Have I slept in?"

"It's ok, go back to sleep. I just wanted to check if you were feeling ok and needed something maybe?" Rosa couldn't believe how much her mother had changed over the last few months. She looked horrible compared to what she was used to. John had explained that her parents were now aging at a more rapid rate. More than the normal person. This frightened Rosa. Mostly because she could see the truth in that with her own eyes. Her parents were changing right in front of her and she knew that it wasn't normal. What worried her most was if they were aging like this how long would they be alive for? Would they age into old people within the next ten years? She loved her parents so much and they were really all she had in this life. She would be lost without them.

"No, I'm fine. Just a bit tired. Did you eat anything yet? I can make you some eggs if you like." Luisa started to sit up.

"No I already ate." This wasn't true but she didn't want her mother to get up just for her. "I'm going to head off to school now."

162

Rosa bent down and gave her mother a kiss on the forehead and headed out of the bedroom. She needed to know they were going to be ok and decided to call John on the way to school, just to be sure.

Later that night John decided to pay a visit to the house. Before Rosa came out of her bedroom he had a quick talk with Giovanni and Luisa about his phone call with Rosa earlier that day.

"She seems to be very worried about you both. She said not only do you look older but you seem to be a bit slower in movement these days. Is there anything else I need to know lately? You didn't come in for the usual checkup last week. Guys, you know how important it is that we keep a consistent record of everything. Can you come by tomorrow maybe?"

Both Giovanni and Luisa were silent at first, neither wanting to respond. Luisa decided to go first. "John, we are scared. It's one thing to not grow old, not to show any signs of aging. That can be scary but not as scary as waking up and looking in the mirror every day to see that you are looking more and more like an old person. It's not gradual at all. I'm waking up with my face dragging to the floor! I bought the creams that normally help the average woman and they work great but on me that only lasts for a day or two. My hair, I can't keep up with the coloring! I have to do it at least every three days. I can't suddenly walk around with so much grey hair. John, people are looking at us funny. We are avoiding the usual events, school events even. I don't know what to do. Giovanni and I were thinking of moving, somewhere different where nobody would notice us and the changes we are going through. I know it would be hard on Rosa but it might be harder on her if people start to talk."

"Where would you go? Really? If you go too far I can't keep an eye on you both. Then what? What if something drastic happens? I want you to know that Cathy and I are willing to take care of Rosa should anything happen to you. I know it's not something you want to hear but I have been wanting to mention this to you and it just never seems to be the right time. I am sure that Michael's family will also be there for her as well. I'm sorry to bring it up."

Giovanni looked intensely at John. "John, that means a lot to us both. If there was anyone we trust with our daughter it would be you and Cathy, hell your entire family. I thank you for the offer. I just hope that it doesn't come to that."

They were all taken back when Rosa entered the room. "Are they dying? Is there something you all aren't telling me?" She was very upset and just stood there looking from one to the other for an answer.

163

Giovanni got up right away. "Rosa sweetheart, no. Nothing is happening to your mother and I, I promise."

"We can't lie to her either Giovanni." Luisa got up and walked toward them both looking straight at Rosa. "You need to know and you need to understand that we don't even know what is happening. But what you should know is that you will never be alone Rosa. Your father and I hope to God that whatever it is that is happening to us right now will either stop or slow down. But we don't know. We can't know! This is new to everyone. Even John." It was this reason that she was glad they told her when they did. How else could they explain what was clearly happening to them to her? If she didn't believe them that night she had to believe them in that moment.

"It's ok, mama. I understand. I'm here to help." She hugged Luisa and then Giovanni.

Chapter 31

Their aging increased but started to slow down once they reached an age that seemed to be close to the mid 70's. Their blood work over time showed that their aging process seemed to go at a double rate than the average person but interestingly, after close to twenty years it stopped and the process returned to a normal aging rate.

Mitchell could no longer work at the lab anymore. He had become bedridden and remained in a daycare facility. John continued to do more research using their DNA make-up with Luisa and Giovanni's consent, knowing how successful he would be. John seemed even more determined than his father was.

Mitchell's death was very hard on the family. He became like a grandfather figure to Rosa. It was yet another hard time for Luisa to go through, another person she had outlived. Mitchell was a huge part of Luisa's life as she transitioned into an independent woman. A large part of her was happy that the aging had begun. She was grateful, however, that it didn't all happen suddenly and they were blessed with what they had already, which was to raise Rosa for twenty years so far. The more years they had the better of course.

But Luisa's losses didn't stop at Mitchell, Michael also passed before her. This was extremely hard for Luisa being Michael was the last of the family she really knew. Although she had Rosa now, Michael was the last connection to the life she had on the vineyard back in California. After Michael's passing, that was all gone now. Her life was so different.

When Rosa turned 27, Luisa passed away in her sleep. She was in no pain at all and Giovanni and Rosa knew it was coming very soon. Luisa made peace with God and herself and looked forward to her next journey. Only two years later, Giovanni passed. Rosa was grateful for her time with her parents. After working with John and his team, she finally understood everything that her parents had told her back when she was thirteen.

Rosa ended up meeting a man that worked on John's team at the laboratory. His name was Mark. He was so impressed with Rosa and of course attracted to her. She turned out to be a beautiful woman. They started to date often and it turned out to be a serious relationship.

Rosa was in her office talking to Mark on the phone when another call came through, it was John.

"Let me talk to you later." She touched a button on her computer, which took the next call. "Hi John, what's going on?"

"Rosa, I need to see you in my office, right away if you can." John sounded strange, not his usual self.

She hurried to his office and knocked on the door. "John?"

"Come in Rosa."

She opened the door slowly not sure what to expect for some reason. John got up from his chair. "Come in, close the door behind you." He went over to his table so that they could both sit down. There, he started to take some documents to show her.

"Look at this. Do you remember when we discovered the breakthrough from your parents DNA? We had the knowledge to have people live as long as they did? Remember? And we decided that it wouldn't be the best idea. Not now anyway."

Rosa was so confused, they had gone over this millions of times before. She knew that at one point John was consumed with this discovery. He wasn't sure what to do with the information. Why was he approaching this again? They both decided what was best. "John we have been through this before - "

He cut her off. "Yes, yes but you see what I did here? I managed to manipulate the structure. Rosa…" John took off his glasses and placed them on the table rubbing his eyes in disbelief. "Rosa, I've tested this over and over and it worked."

"What worked John?"

"It cured the cancer cells."

Rosa felt that time stood still for a second. Why didn't she even realize this is what he was going to tell her. Her parents told her all about the story but there was a big part of her that didn't believe it was going to happen. Especially because it hadn't already. Apprehension gripped her. Did this mean that everything her parents had told her was true? She was going to return to the past? Her entire future changed from this point on and she knew it was now time to tell John everything she knew.

A few years later John had won the noble prize for his discovery. Rosa stood right beside him, prouder than ever. They both knew who it was that they owed this to but it was just between themselves.

One day, Rosa came knocking on John's office. John was still in charge of everything but Rosa advanced pretty quickly, climbing the scientific ladder, her focus on biology and time theory providing her with a unique resume. John wasn't sure how much longer he would be around to guide the research on Luisa and Giovanni, and mentored Rosa as closely as he could.

"Hi Rosa, how are you today? What's up?" John had her sit down.

"Everything is good. Actually, really good. John, as you know, I've been seeing Mark for some time now. I think it's serious. We talk a lot about our future."

"Mark is a good man. I'm glad to hear it. Smart too. Is there a problem? Do you need help with anything?" John now was curious where this conversation was going. Ever since Giovanni and Luisa passed, he looked after Rosa along with Michael's family. Although John and Mitchell felt more like family than Michael's.

"Oh everything is fine. I was just thinking, with Mark working here and everything, I feel that perhaps I should I let him in on my parents and the work that you and I have done? I mean maybe not right now of course but what if I were to marry him one day? Shouldn't he know?"

"No. Rosa, we cannot take that chance and you have to trust me with this. I know it's not what you want to hear. Believe me, all my life I had to hide all of this from my family. They never knew. Think of it as work that you don't share with your loved ones because it's boring. Yes, in this case it is far from boring. It's extraordinary but we can't. Just you and I can only know about the research and about your task one day. If your future self had said he knew I would support that decision, but she didn't. So you mustn't take the chance."

She understood and promised not to say a word.

Chapter 32

2104

The room was very cold and Rosa wished she had dressed a little warmer. She had recently turned 85 and the older she got the colder she seemed to be.

"Mrs. Meyers, we are ready for you now." A woman in a white jumpsuit entered the doorway of the room Rosa had been waiting in. "I'm Alina," the woman said.

She got up and followed the woman down a hallway that was brightly lit, the walls and floors immaculately cleaned. There was just the two of them. You could hear the woman's shoes clicking on the floor as they walked down the hallway.

Alina looked at Rosa and smiled. "Everyone is very excited about this. Are you ok?"

Rosa was indeed a bit nervous but she wasn't going to let that show and assured her she was fine.

At the end of the hall was a large steel door. They both entered into a room with ten people rushing from machine to machine making sure all the final steps were completed. Each station was filled with blinking lights, floating around the room in constant rotation. Rosa couldn't believe how far things had come since she was young. There were no more computers on desks. Everything just floated in the air and appeared with voice activation following each person as they walked around the room. Technology had surpassed anything she could imagine and yet she was about to go to a time that a telephone would be magical. She prepared herself for this journey, knowing that life would be harder with so much less technology then what she was used to. The last thirty years Rosa made sure not to rely so much on all the advancements that were out there. She knew all about them but made sure to get used to doing things the old-fashioned way, too. She researched how life was during the early 1900's and worked on different skill sets, and her Italian so that when she arrived in the past she would be prepared for what greeted her.

She was the first to test traveling back in time. As soon as she found out what team was working on time travel she got herself involved, shaking her resume at them. She was able to offer financial help to them as long as she was the first to test it. They told her that they had not figured out a way to return – she didn't even blink, just asked where to report.

She was guided into a separate glass paneled room. Inside was what resembled a hospital bed – the room was perfectly sterile. They all helped her get comfortable on it. She wore a simple plain dress and had a small carrying bag with her. It was all she could take. There was a maximum weight allowed and the less she had the better they felt about depositing her in the correct time.

Rosa laid down and relaxed. She looked up at the ceiling that was at least three stories high. Directly above her was a dome, steel contraption.

"Now, just relax. Everything will be fine," a man assured her.

Rosa sat back, remembering how her parents told her what it was she had to do. Everything in her life was scripted for her. She wondered what would happen had she decided to take another route. What if she decided not to work with Mitchell's son? If she just left after the death of her parents and lived a very different life. More importantly, what if she did not return to save her parents? Would she just disappear into thin air? What would actually happen to everyone that her parents were in contact with? Without them, the laboratory would never be in existence. She herself would not exist, but here she was. She already lived her life, how can that be taken back when she had the memories already in her head? The only answer she could think of was that she must have done what was needed in order for all of this to be real. What if she got up right now and left the building? What would happen?

She asked these questions to John not too long ago. He told her he could not answer her questions with a correct answer. How could he possibly know himself? He guessed that perhaps if she did not go back and save her parents that this life was really taking place in another dimension. A "what if" place. There could possibly be many different scenarios happening all over the universe.

She asked him what would happen if she prevented the fire from starting in the first place. They both came to the same conclusion, Rosa would not exist therefore her parents would not have been around for Mitchell to make any discovery at all. It was so strange when you thought about it. It was like asking which came first, the chicken or the egg.

A huge fan above her started to slowly rotate making a very loud noise in the room, which made it hard to hear.

"Everything will be fine! Just relax and close your eyes!" the technician assured her, yelling over the fan. He then stepped out of the room and dimmed the lights.

Rosa tried her best to relax. She took deep breaths and envisioned a time with her parents in the park when she was about ten years old. Those were very happy times for her. She couldn't wait to see them again. They told her nothing of her time back in the 1900's. Everything must come naturally, as Giovanni assured her. The only thing they said was that she must somehow get them to take a pill each right after they were pulled out of the fire.

It then suddenly occurred to her. The pills. Rosa's eyes opened quickly but it was too late. A beam of light came from every direction.

Chapter 33

While Rosa was being transported, two women were cleaning up the room that Rosa had been waiting in before she traveled back. They did not know what was going on in the rest of the building although they did know most of it was top secret. All they did was their job.

One of the women walked over to the end table where Rosa had used a paper cup for water. As she went to throw the cup out, she noticed a tiny plastic bag next to the cup along with a package of tissues.

"Look, the poor old lady left her medicine here." She held it up to her co-worker. In it contained three white pills.

"I'm sure she has a bottle of them back at home. You might as well just throw them away," the other woman responded.

The plastic cup and pills were put into the garbage can. The tissues she decided to keep in her pocket.

1879

The night my grandmother died was one of the worst memories for me. We all stood around her in her final moments. Being the grandchild that seemed the closest to Nonna, I was the one who was able to hold her hand. I remember her eyes slowly opening as she tilted her head down and looked at me. She somehow managed to nod her head as if to tell me everything was going to be ok. She pursed her lips slightly as if to kiss me. Then she took her last breath.

Then there was silence, a long heavy moment before those surrounding her sniffed and sobbed. The pain was unbearable. I quickly got up brushing past my mother who tried to console me and ran out back throwing open the doors to the outside. It was a warm night and the sun was just about to set. All I could see in the distance was the vineyards, which were black with shadows – an orange sky glowing angrily behind it. I got down on my knees and looked up to the clouds folding my hands together.

"Please God, I never wish this on anyone. Please, let me live forever so that my children and grandchildren never have to

171

experience my death and be as heartbroken as I am now! Please promise me I will live a very long life."